Tales From The Murenger

Stories to darken the soul

MICHAEL KEYTON

Copyright © 2017 Michael Keyton

All rights reserved.

ISBN: 154272337X
ISBN-13: 978-1542723374

Cover Art by Maria Zannini
Photograph by Monty Dart

DISCLAIMER

Names, characters, and incidents depicted in this book are products of the author's imagination or are used fictitiously. Any resemblance to actual events, or persons, living or dead, is entirely coincidental and beyond the intent of the author.

EDICATION

To the Murenger, the 'Pub of Dreams' and those who value its magic, Maria Zannini for her generosity and unswerving support, Veronica Sicoe for her kindness and technical expertise and to my wife and children for everything that's important in my life.

Contents

1	Mr. Nousel's Mirror	11
2	Flesh	26
3	Martin Brownlow's Cat	39
4	Housebound	51
5	Beside The Seaside, Beside The Sea	67
6	Bony Park	79
7	Tom Baxter	83
8	A Touch of Rat	91
9	Such A Night	103
10	Raggedy Man	110
11	The Devil's Mirror	131
12	Senectus	141
13	Ailsa	153
	About The Author	169
	Other Titles	170

*Newport is a dark, seedy and magical city,
the unimaginable just around the next corner...
or the one after that.*

Mr. Housel's Mirror

I have always thought there is more to the lanes surrounding the market than meets the eye.

I remember pausing, the tall medieval lines of the car park on my left; to my right the King's Head, a late Victorian hotel: red bricks, deep windows and sandstone sills laced in grime. Facing me were the grey ruins of Newport castle. I paused an instant longer, content to allow the thoughtless bustle pass me by. A wind, cold and gritty, scattered paper across the pavement, causing my eyes to water and fading everything into a washed-out blur.

I checked the map once more, then retraced my steps, stopping before a narrow street that ran down the side of the market. The street was strangely silent as if for some reason people chose to avoid it, perhaps had good reason to. I shivered, sensing that it wasn't the kind of place to linger when darkness fell. Though I walked slowly, my footsteps seemed abnormally loud, almost as if the enclosed space were savouring the sound, savouring my presence. Then I saw it, a tiny arcade to my left, an alley, a winding thread, grimy and underused.

Unobtrusive doorways, silent in dust, appeared on either side of me, and before each one I paused, studying signs, fading labels or any other indication as to what the rooms above might hold. A door that had once been painted green came into view. It was half-open, and below a knocker cast in the form of a seedy-looking lion was a small brass plate. Dr. William Nousel—Optics.
I sighed then in some relief, and cautiously walked up a flight of grey wooden stairs. They led to a landing and four facing doors, all but one of them closed. I hesitated, resting my hand on a crudely carved balustrade and stared at the one partially opened door. It was barely ajar, its rectangular silhouette outlined in a thin seam of light. Someone was on the other side, listening, and I wondered whether he had picked up my footfall in the alley, perhaps even the street beyond.

"Mr. Nousel?" The question was accompanied by a tentative knock.

"Mr. James. Come in. I've been expecting you." There was relief in the voice, even perhaps eagerness that caused me again to hesitate. I pushed the street-map deep down into my pocket, and tightened my grip on a neatly furled newspaper. It was an instinctive gesture, as if the baton shaped paper might in some way serve as an explanation, or subliminal threat. The thought made me grin. I clutched it firmly and opened the door wide.

The room beyond was bathed in a golden light and belonged to a different age. It exuded careless opulence, shabby, scholarly even arcane. A large Persian rug almost hidden in books, strewn at random or arranged in towers like termite nests, seemed curiously dominated by a figure hunched expectantly in a chair too large for him. I stared at Mr. Nousel's bone white face and the unnatural brass appendages that looked as if they were glued to his eyes.

A gentle cough prompted me to speak. "I was intrigued by your advert, sir."

"Ah, the 'The Beacon'—you will have come from Monmouth, then." Mr. Nousel stared at the paper for a moment or two. He raised his head, until the two small brass cylinders were aimed directly at my face. Though highly polished they looked strangely crude and yet imbued with the minute and subtle craftsmanship I had learnt to associate with the early eighteenth century, perhaps earlier. And then, to my unease, I became aware of Mr. Nousel's eyes staring out from them, like a pair of large and blue exotic fish.

"Sit down, sit down." Mr. Nousel gestured towards the fire as if suggesting immolation was just the thing on such a cold and blustery day. I edged round books that seemed to be teetering in stasis and dust; there was a sense of tracing time through a labyrinth, the unstable towers now resembling wind-torn buttes as they picked up the glow from the fire.

The chair faced my host, but was positioned closer to the hearth, forcing Mr. Nousel to turn ever so slightly. The effect was off-putting. The brass eyepiece gleamed, and ruddy shadows flowed from his waxen face as if they didn't belong there. Eyes that had only a moment ago appeared as large cobalt fish had been replaced by two tiny red flickers, simulacra of the low burning fire.

Mr. Nousel leant forward and smiled. "I am selling everything—everything," he repeated. "Books, everything in this room, the room itself, if that's what you want." He paused, his smile for a moment sardonic. "And these of course." He tapped the metallic appendages that covered his eyes. I wondered how easily they might be detached. "The Alchemical Lenses, John Dee's last and greatest secret."

I gazed absently across the finally paneled room, glancing once or twice at this or that pile of books, noticing, that for all its subtle richness, the room itself possessed only one tiny window, and that it looked out upon a yellow-brick wall, built only inches away. I kept my voice even, tried to restrain an almost overpowering sense of excitement.

"John Dee, you say." I looked with polite interest at the two cylinders that seemed to grow almost organically from Mr. Nousel's head, and which were pointing at me now like two tiny brass cannons. "They look of later workmanship."

Mr. Nousel nodded approvingly. "So, it *is* the lenses you are after." He sighed, a strange sound of relief and regret. "And your surmise is correct. They were fashioned some years after Dr. Dee's death."

I leant back in my seat, demolishing an adjacent tower block and causing me to wonder whether all of them were attached to each other by a finely spun web of air, and whether very shortly they would all proceed to tumble like synchronised dominoes in a Japanese-run tournament. I raised an eyebrow in way of apology, but my host appeared not to have noticed. Cautiously I repositioned myself, trying once more to disguise any show of excitement.

Ten years or more of study, hunting down every antiquarian reference, every church-yard clue, the thread growing gradually stronger, the scent more intense, so that towards the end I was occasionally prone to the uncomfortable feeling that I was being reeled in; the predator become the eager fish. And now here they were, within arm's length, a mere grasp away. I wondered how much he wanted for them, and whether it would not be easier just to take them. Then I realised the old man was still talking.

"You see both Dee, and later Ashmole of course, believed in angels, faeries, the otherworld, call it what you will." Mr. Nousel sighed. "Only much of Dee's work vanished in flame, and even more of his work perished by virtue of being buried... for safe-keeping"

"Sir Robert Cotton dug some of it up I believe."

"Some of it, sir, some of it." Mr Nousel chuckled. It was a grim sound. Like a mole briefly amused by a worm's repartee. "But you must remember, Mr. James, that a mere breath of wind separated alchemy from sorcery, and for one you could be burned."

"Hanged," The correction was gentle, reflexive. Mr Nousel seemed unperturbed. He waved a hand as if swatting a fly.

"Even so, the most secret part of his work was retrieved, as Dee intended, and was passed down and talked of—discreetly, amongst friends and those who followed similar trails. Ashmole knew of it as, too, did Newton—along with his colleague John Wickens."

I chose my words carefully. Don't give too much away. "I have heard of Wickens. He died, I believe, at Stoke Edith, a few miles or so north of Monmouth."

Mr. Nousel nodded as if the news in no way surprised him. "Ah, the by-ways of Monmouthsire, a natural haunt of alchemists and recusants." He looked up sharply, his glasses twinkling in the light from the fire. "Men who strived to reach other and better worlds."

"As do we all," I said.

He looked at me and licked dry lips. "The magical tradition is powerful, though secretive, and it always exacts a price. Even Sir Isaac cavilled at that—in the end."

"Newton was a great explorer, he dabbled in alchemy, I know." I was finding it increasingly difficult to wrest my gaze far from Mr. Nousel's bone-white face.

"Dabbled! Dabbled, you say." Mr. Nousel leant further forward. "Sir Isaac Newton walked a very thin line, young man. On the one hand he ran the risk of offending the leading alchemists of his day. They were right to be suspicious of him, right to suspect that he would steal their credit. On the other hand he couldn't afford to offend religious conformity—nor the university authorities that patronised him."

"So what did he do?" And when do we get down to talking money? Impatience began to taint a natural interest in the lenses' provenance. I stared guilelessly at the old man, restraining the impulse to just reach out and wrench the alchemical eyepiece from his wretched face. No, no need for that; besides, I knew there were still secrets yet to be voiced; secrets perhaps as vital as the eyepiece itself.

"Newton realised that so long as he didn't actually publish the darker side of his research there would be little if any recrimination, but his experiments continued alongside more orthodox research in to such things as the nature of light." Nousel paused, as if somehow he had just given me a clue and was waiting for it to be taken up.

"So, when Newton would wax lyrical about how light could be manipulated into its various colours then made to converge back into its original whiteness..."

Nousel nodded. "He was also exploring the possibility of its opposite, something more than the mere absence of light."

"Black light, you mean?" It was the wildest of guesses, or else the room and its occupant was slowly, subtly re-configuring my mind. I wondered how much the old man already knew, or sensed about my intentions.

Mr. Nousel smiled. "Black light, a nonsense in how we see things I know." He tapped his eyepiece, "but not impossible. You see, both he and Wickens speculated on the nature of the space that separated the colours. Both of them believed there was more behind what our eyes allow us to see."

An image came suddenly into my mind, causing me to shudder. Something I had read at school. "He nearly blinded himself—Newton. I read that somewhere."

"On more than one occasion. Staring into the sun in search of perfect blackness." Nousel coughed as if he had just made a joke and was pleased with it. "In his notes he described it as a study in eye fatigue. Again, some time later, he proceeded to press a bodkin deep between his eye and its bony cavity. Pressing it just behind the optic nerve and analysing the black and white circles he created by varying the pressure. Curiosity, Mr. James, and a peculiar sense of duty."

Mr. Nousel spoke slowly, clearly sensing and enjoying my evident discomfort. "In the end, however, Newton found his fame in more orthodox pursuits. It was the incomparable Wickens who built upon the dreams of Ashmole, Wickens who explored the clues that Dr. Dee had made obscure. John Wickens who manufactured these." He tapped the strange spectacles once more.

"And you would sell them—to me?"

Nousel sighed, again with that strange mixture of relief and regret. "Are you a dutiful man, Mr. James?" He didn't wait for an answer. "Come back tomorrow and we might agree a price."

I stared into the bone-white face and knew that I would. The face was expressionless, putting me in mind of a gambler saving his best card until last.

As I stood up to leave, I spotted the mirror behind me, just to the right of the door.

That night I dreamed of the mirror. I remember walking towards it, knowing that should I see my reflection, I might never wake up. To my relief the mirror was black; it reminded me of an oriel window looking out upon a starless night. As I walked closer, the mirror thickened into something gelatinous and black, and I sensed in it the reptilian, the cold, unblinking stare of something on the other side. The feeling was so strong I imagined I saw it coiling towards me, and then the picture fragmented into the sinuous writhing of what looked like coffin worms. Only as I approached did I see that they were in fact women, white and naked and extending back into the mirror as far as the eye could see. They looked upon me with eyes that were both languorous and bold, and I wondered what further marvels lay beyond.

I returned early the next morning, a cheque neatly folded in my middle pocket, confident that come what may a transaction of one kind or another would take place, and then I wondered what Mr. Nousel would do with the money.

The street seemed even more silent that morning, my footsteps a little louder. As I passed the various doors, I pictured a Mr. Nousel, sitting patiently behind each one, all of them waiting to make a sale.

But Mr. Nousel's door was open; even the seedy lion appeared to be smiling at me today. I stroked the tarnished knocker almost proprietarily and marched briskly up the grey wooden stairway.

"Ah, Mr. James." The greeting was warm, the fire just a little warmer. As I walked in, I became aware on an intense fragrance like that of an orchid coming into bloom. And then I remembered the mirror. My glance was casual and brief, necessarily so, since most of my attention was focussed on manoeuvring past the random columns of books. I noticed that, as in my dream, the mirror offered little in the way of reflection; the smell, too, seemed to be coming from that part of the room.

"Sit down. Sit down."

The old man had cleared a pathway through the maze of books separating the two chairs: a sign perhaps that he, too, was eager to get down to business.

"I would like to buy it from you." I waved my arm carelessly across the littered study, trying to convey an air of the omnivorous collector. "Everything in fact."

"Even the mirror?"

"Especially the mirror." The answer seemed to come

from nowhere, as if my mind somehow sensed more than it could shape into words. I remembered the dream, and knew that both the mirror and the eyepiece were fundamentally linked. Even so, it had been a mistake to sound so eager. Was I really prepared to pay more than was needed? Mr. Nousel smiled, and I noticed that the two brass cylinders gleamed even more brightly than the day before, as if the old man had polished them especially for the occasion.

"It will not come cheap." Mr. Nousel said, as if somehow guessing my thoughts. "None of it will, but let me tell you more, and then you can tell me whether you are still interested."

"You said that they were manufactured by Wickens and that he in turn was working on principles established by Dee." I paused, largely for effect. "And now you seem to be hinting that the eye-glass is somehow linked with the mirror standing behind me." I glanced round at the dense pool of blackness defined by a tall rectangular frame. "In any event I will make you richer than any man needs to be in order to have them both."

"Along with their history of course," said the old man imperturbably. "Else you may be buying more or less than you expected."

Curiosity helped curb my impatience. I was about to buy a secret, something that would shake reality into fragments. I wondered how and why it had been kept a secret for so long and why, now, the old man was about to sell it.

"You see," Mr, Nousel continued. "John Dee questioned what Newton would later seek. What else might be seen if light could be refracted through the Philosopher's Stone?"

"The Philosopher's Stone." The neutral tone failed to disguise my disappointment. He'd be talking about Dracula next, the Da Vinci Code, Harry Potter. I closed my eyes, examining the possibility that I had just crashed into yet another dead end. It was irrational I knew, to have pursued almost obsessively the workings of minds such as Ashmole,

Wickens and Dee, and at the same time to hesitate over one of their central beliefs.

Mr. Nousel chuckled. "I see the phrase creates doubt. The magic shatters about you, the power of words, eh."

The power of words indeed, I thought, angry at my own irrationality. How many times had I argued that magic might contain answers to abstruse quantum puzzles? It was all a matter of words. Scientists conjectured extra dimensions but had as yet found none, for all their talk of high energy and short-distance observation. Words. Our reality was probably little more than a fluke, a tiny three-dimensional pocket inside a universe of infinite variants. And inside this room was the alchemical secret that would reveal what science couldn't. Believe it, believe. I believed and smiled, and thought of Tinkerbelle, dying in an airless vase.

"Something amuses you."

"I'm sorry. Truth sometimes wears unfashionable clothes, I know."

"Words date, the truth does not—quite so." Mr. Nousel leant forward. "And have you in your studies come across the 'Prospective Stone'?"

"I have heard of it."

"Only our old friend Elias Ashmole writes about it with great enthusiasm—great enthusiasm. Through it, he believed it would be possible to discover any person—" Mr. Nousel raised his face to the ceiling, giving me the distinct impression that his eyes were closed, and that he was quoting directly from pages seen only in his head. "—in any part of the world whatsoever, although never so secretly concealed or hid in chambers, closets or caverns of the earth. In a word, it fairly presents to your view even the whole world, wherein to behold, hear, or see your desire. And yet this I assure you is not in anyways necromantical or devilish; but easy, wondrous easy, natural and honest."

I regarded the optical device greedily. "The Prospective stone is incorporated in that?" I tried to make a joke. "Beats Google Earth, I suppose or anything else the Americans have."

"Oh, it's more than that, Martin," Mr. Nousel said gently. "It is much more than that." He raised his hands to his face as if about to take the device off, then thought better of it. He tapped it instead. "Here, light is refracted through *two* stones, subtly cut and layered in most ingenious ways. You will have heard, too, of the Angelical stone, Mr. James, or else I suspect you would not be here now."

I nodded, content to be silent. The time for pretence was past. The wizard Dee had talked with angels, but he'd always wanted more, and here in this room was what he had striven for but never lived to see: entrance to their world.

"It is the stone that Wickens and Ashmole valued above anything else, and as I said, they discovered clues to its making in Dee's most secret writings."

"Only Ashmole died."

The bone-white face nodded. "But that unsung genius of the alchemical art, John Wickens continued the work, at first in collaboration with Newton then later alone in the obscurity of Stoke Edith." He tapped the eyepiece once more. "And here you have the two stones, translucent and layered, catching light and unseen worlds in the most subtle of prisms."

"The Angelical Stone," I whispered.

Nousel smiled, as if the two of us were just then sharing a glass of the world's finest wine. "Something that can be neither seen, felt or weighed, a thing less visible than air yet possessing great power—"

"—Affording sight of Angels—the power of conversing with them in dream and revelation. Yes, I have read of it. But the mirror—what about the mirror?"

"Ah, the mirror you will see soon enough, but as to what you will pay—"

"I will pay what you ask."

"You may change your mind."

Something in his tone made me uneasy. I remembered a circus, a five-year-old boy, and how a clown, hideously white and bald with black painted eyes had pushed his face close to my own and pushed out his tongue. I had screamed. I remember my father laughing.

Mr Nousel didn't laugh, but he frightened me more. "Wickens found something he shouldn't."

"The mirror..."

"Less a mirror than a window that can never be shut." Mr. Nousel lowered his head as if the eyepiece had become suddenly heavy. "It is why he made these."

I turned, staring into the mirror I'd dreamed of that night.

"In it is magic, pure and evil. More than our world could hold." There was a curious longing in his voice as one already seduced.

"I don't understand."

"I am 'A Watcher' Mr. James, as you will be. My eyes veil the window, engages the rift. It feeds on my mind, and is unaware of any world beyond."

"The finger in the dyke... but why?" I stared around the room, realising again how small it was.

"The mirror is addictive. What might occupy a world captures a mind. It quickly discovers what you most desire... and satisfies. And when it is done feeding ... it takes you."

"You want to be taken?"

"Oh, yes, I want to be taken."

"After a new 'Watcher' releases you..." I wondered how many there'd been. "You could just smash it."

"And create a hundred thousand windows." He smiled sadly. "Are you having second thoughts?"

Yes, yes, I wanted to run... and yet. "If you're so desperate," I nodded at the mirror. "Why sell it?"

"You mean give it away?" The smile turned sour

"Sometimes I think it is the mirror that chooses... it senses the curious."

Mr Nousel pulled himself to his feet and brought his face closer. "But do you believe in duty, Martin? Duty. Do you believe in that?" Slowly he raised both hands to the gleaming brass, and even more slowly tugged, stretching unnaturally white skin until I half expected to see it tear free from the bone. There followed one final soft, reluctant squelch as the eyeglasses released their hold on long dead flesh.

For one horrible moment I didn't know whether to retch or scream. I turned, determined then to flee the room, but caught sight of the mirror and knew then I'd been caught.

"Mr. James." The old man sounded as if he were in pain. His head was bowed and he held the magical artifice in both hands like a vassal to a king. "Take them before it's too late."

Too late—what did he mean? I hesitated, turning instinctively towards the door as the old man looked up. There was a whiff of corrupted flesh, a smell like that of very old meat. I glimpsed ruined eyes, thin, like tiny blue maggots wriggling franticall, things seeking the dark.

"What do you mean, before it's too late?"

"The lenses they need a host." The old man spoke in short, measured gasps. He was staring at the mirror like a man about to jump from a very high building.

"And you think I want to pay its price?"

"Yes," he said, "I do. You have spent your life searching for this, Mr. James. And now you have found it." Mr. Nousel's voice softened. "Dee's Angelic Realms." He pushed the eyepiece closer to my face. "Your every desire satisfied. Take them. The price is what you are prepared to pay." His tone became intimate, like a salesman closing a deal. "Just try them, look into the mirror and then tell me you're not interested."

"You mean I can take them off as and when I please?"

"Oh yes, Mr. James, as and when you please."

I took the eyepiece from him and brought it slowly up to my face. The polished brass retained a lingering smell of rotten meat, forcing me at once to hold it at some distance from my nose. It was as I was fishing out a handkerchief from an inside pocket that I heard a soft mewling sound. I looked up to see Mr. Nousel slowly careering round the room, whimpering like a kitten in pain. Both hands were fixed to his head and he was shaking it slowly from side to side.

"Mr. Nousel!" Books tumbled in ruined piles as the old man weaved his way clumsily towards the gloomy mirror. The thought came from nowhere. Smash it! Smash it! As for the eyepiece - I looked at the finely engineered brass in horror and disgust and felt my face convulse at the thought of what being a 'watcher' entailed. I reached for one of two paperweights resting on a small table, then looking up, froze.

The old man had reached the mirror, was touching its surface, was walking through, the blackness closing in around him like ink, or fine silk. I caught a glimpse of Nousel's half turned face, twisted in longing and lust, saw his lips move, "They're waiting for me." The syllables disappearing like bubbles in a pond. And then I heard a faint, high-pitched scream—of ecstasy—or fear, followed by silence.

I leapt towards the dark mirror, causing books to crash in all directions. I hurled myself at it with force, confident that I too, would pass through into what lay behind. The glass should have shattered. Instead it held firm, and however hard I pushed and poked or prodded there seemed no evident entry through it into another more exotic world. However hard I stared, and from whatever angle, it offered nothing but the dimmest reflection, as if it had sucked up all the light in the room, and enough was enough.

Then I regarded the brass eyepiece. It dangled loosely in my hand, its gleam an enticing wink. I stared at it for a moment or two longer. A decade of research, obsessive at times, reduced to this: revulsion and temptation, fear and desire. The mirror looked back at me, as if somehow it knew what I would do.

Decision made, but not knowing whose it was, a fearsome thought possessed me. Even if I stopped the horror beyond would I in turn become part of it, my mind and soul consumed until like Nousel it snapped me up as a dry little fly? I wondered whether this was the fate of every 'Watcher'. Were we making it stronger, our sacrifices ultimately in vain?

I licked dry lips and returned to Nousel's chair on legs of warm jelly. The mirror's smell had become more intense, filling the room with a perfume of rose and rotten meat, and its glass rippled then slowly bulged, as though the thing behind had sensed an open door.

I held the eyepiece firmly and raised it to my head.

FLESH

> *Old Newport is riddled with interconnected cellars, long forgotten tunnels, and below those...*

eter walked on, occasionally looking behind him. It wasn't a good part of Newport to be in, especially at night. Still, he was there. He had found it.

The take-away was crimson lit, but he could see little else through windows grey in steam and blurred with rain, just the red neon sign: 'Moccus'. Peter hesitated. From inside came a low murmuring.

He stepped in quickly despite the sweet, greasy smell. The room was long and dark in shadow, the murmuring now a loud and contented mumble.

The sound disturbed him, and he walked without appetite to a counter framed in crimson light. He weaved his way through rust-coloured gobblers, tried to blank out the sound of jaws chomping on gristle and fat. For the first time he wished he'd taken up waste disposal, mortuary work, anything but this job.

The counter looked clean enough, the man behind less

so. Peter scanned the wall menu, glanced at the meat glistening on its revolving stand and ordered a Doner Kebab.

"How did you find us?"

Peter started. So officialdom had a smell. He stared at the man, noticing for the first time how thin he was, and red like pepperoni. His shadow, looming on the wall behind, was that of someone larger.

Hygiene was the least of it. There'd been rumours of bush-meat and meat that had once worn collars. Rumours. Peter grimaced. What he was doing here at this time of night was over and above the call of duty. Well, at least he had found the place.

"Who told you?" Pepperoni sliced the meat carefully, avoiding Peter's gaze.

Peter shrugged. "Is that important?" *He was a customer, nothing more.* He wished he hadn't come, had left it until morning and made it official.

Pepperoni smiled, a dark slash across the face. He handed over a large kebab and a cold can of coke. "On the house." As Peter reached the door a low, sepulchral voice urged him to 'Enjoy.'

Enjoy... The kebab was hot in his hand and glowed invitingly beneath the sodium glare of the single lamppost. A bin was attached to it but the glistening meat promised succulence, and the night was cold. He raised the meat to his lips, breathed in its smell. *One bite ... and then the bin.*

The strangeness began when Peter was walking up Bridge Street. He leant against the plate glass of a solicitor's office, waiting for the dizziness to pass.

As he stood, the ground yawned before him, opening into a large hollow that deepened into a funnel of darkness. Its sides had a bluish tinge and, as he focussed, it seemed as if he were looking down the inside of a vast conical hat made from a rich fabric of blues merging into grey. There were subtle folds in the sides, whether of shadow or faint indentations, he couldn't be sure, and soaring towards him from the inverted apex of the hollow, a tall street, its houses silvery in half-light and separated by the narrowest of lanes.

It was a street of weirdly carved gables, of thin windows, mullioned and tallow lit. It was a street of chimneys, skeletal and crooked, silhouetted against a darkening sky. And as he watched, the windows slowly opened, and from them creatures, sharp and malformed, stared up at him. Sallow and slant of eye, long chinned and narrow of face; some with noses as long as their chins; the hobgoblins gazed at him through eyes that glittered like small polished beetles. He wondered whether it was the drink or the Kebab, and then staggered as the ground beneath him collapsed taking him down into the nightmarish street below.

He landed on cobbles, and found himself looking up at the overhanging windows; and from them faces stared back, curious, their long chins resting on steepled fingers. There was an expectancy about them that made him uneasy, and his gaze shifted to the far end of the street, where a shadow moved purposefully towards him. He swivelled to find the path behind him blocked by a wall.

Peter scanned the impossibly thin houses on either side each separated by a fine line of shadow, as much a crack as a lane. A quick glance at the gaunt creature now almost upon him jolted his senses, and he dived into the nearest crack and blackness.

She spoke in a sibilant lilt, her hands soft, perfumed and greasy. Peter felt other hands, tentative hands, all exploratory, some touching, others sliding up his leg and thigh. He tried to move but apart from his head and an urgently questing penis, he remained immobile. No sense of chain, or straps or rope. Nothing tactile pressed against him. But he couldn't move, only his penis, straining for take-off.

Peter opened his eyes. A bald woman with large oriental eyes stared back at him and smiled. Her left hand, thumb and palm were cupped against his jaw. Her right hand was pressing something into the side of his head just above the ear.

"Did you offend him?" Her voice, slightly husky, had a bird-song cadence.

"Who?"

"Moccus."

"I don't know. My name is Johnson, Pete Johnson."

"Jonssonpetejonsson." His name echoed around him in sounds reminiscent of an aviary. Suddenly free, he pulled himself into a sitting position; hands rippled from him like fish in a panic.

He turned, looking for clues, wondering whether he was in hospital or somewhere more sinister, but there was nothing, no furniture, no walls nor windows, no doors. Instead, he was surrounded by women all of them eerily alike, and all of them naked, their bodies glistening in oil or a second, transparent skin.

Their heads were smooth, their bodies small, and when he stood, none of them stood higher than his chest. Then he realised *he* was naked, too, and all of them were staring at him with their large sloe eyes, their attention focussed on his rapidly shrinking penis.

"I am Niko."

It was the smooth-headed oriental who spoke, the woman who had awoken him. He stared at her, absorbing every aspect of her face in his gaze. And then she smiled, and he noted that hers was the low and husky voice.

A flicker of annoyance crossed her face and he turned, confronting her twin who was now standing so close to him he could smell her breath. *Little concept of body space then.* The thought excited him.

He breathed in her smell of honey and almond, aware that she was looking at his wavering penis. And then she lifted her head and smiled. *Damn. Identical face... No, not quite.* Her eyes possessed none of Niko's warmth; here was detachment. He was being analysed. And her mouth, though smiling, seemed sly.

"Why did you offend him?" Her voice had the same birdsong cadence but more hard.

Because he was about to be closed down. "I don't know."

"You are not being helpful." The birdsong was now sharp.

"Cassy is unduly direct, Jonssonpetejonsson." It was Niko with her husky voice. He turned to be greeted by warmth. She was smiling, and amusement flickered in her eyes. *Yes, I like Niko.* He decided to trust her... to trust all of them. He had no choice.

A brief, disorientating glance round showed him he was surrounded—more than surrounded, immersed, in a wriggling pattern of women writhing in obsidian darkness like hieroglyphs come to life. It was as though he stood in some vast black ocean without bottom or surface and all around, glistening figures arranging themselves in a loose but intimate amphitheatre with himself, Niko and Cassy at its centre.

Trust them? Stupid... stupid! It's some kind of nightmare... if not... No he wouldn't go down there. *Play for time. Must have been something in the kebab. Hallucinogenic. Scrawny red-faced bastard. I'll be lying somewhere in Bridge Street. Ambulance... I'll hear the sirens any minute now... relax... relax. Say something, anything at all.* "My friends call me Peter, Pete."

"Peterpete."

"No just Pete. And I live in Newport..." *Wales, Britain, Europe, the world, the universe... where do I go from here?* "A... a... different world."

Cassy, in front of him now and shoulder to shoulder with Niko, smiled sardonically. "A different world... you think so?"

"So why did Moccus send you here? The questions had the relentless force of hail on grass, and he bowed his head wondering how he would answer.

"He is tired," said Cassy.

"Thirsty," said Nico.

Before he'd had time to answer a woman, shapely but equally diminutive, , pressed a large beaker of sweet liquid to his lips. The taste exploded in his mouth like a mixture of rocket fuel and sherbet. He gulped it, and his insides tingled in a soothing chill. As if guessing his needs, the child-woman offered him another, and he would have gone for a third had not Cassy coughed and gently pushed the child away. Again, there was that hint of annoyance in Niki's eyes. She didn't appear to like Cassy much either, and that was fine by him.

"Cassy, our guest must be tired." The voice was smooth, imperious, brooking no argument.

Cassy's body tensed, and her lips tightened into something that wasn't a smile.

"We shall talk again soon." There was a gleam in Niko's eyes, the voice a little more husky. Peter nodded, sensing possibilities but too tired to conjecture exactly what. His head felt numb, and he took Cassy's hand and followed where she led.

It was like walking through an interminable sponge. There was a richness to the air, a texture, warm, almost like jelly. After a time it was hard to know whether they were moving up or down, or when they turned. The purpled darkness simply absorbed them as they walked. Sometimes women, as identical as whitebait, slipped by, moving with a furtive grace, their glistening bodies sliding through the richness like oiled silverfish. And for the first time he became aware of a heavy, almost overpowering scent.

Something else troubled him. He should have asked the question earlier. He asked it now. "Where are the men?" Cassy turned, her answer slow in coming. "You should be asleep... Two draughts of Meibra were more than enough."

"Just as well I'm not then—we haven't found a bed yet."

"A bed? You sleep where you lie, Jonssonpetejonsson." She looked at him speculatively. "So, you are not tired?"

Peter regarded her. "No, just numb—that was strong stuff."

"She should not have given it to you so soon. You have still much to learn."

Sour-puss. "So are there men here?" For a moment he allowed himself to dream—what if there was no competition—and would he get to like women without hair?

"There are men here, but those we keep are rare and so precious. To own one is the highest of honours."

"So that was why they were all staring at my dick?" He didn't know why he was being so offensive. With Niko he would have made the effort... but Cassy, well he'd met her kind before, sour, judgemental and as dry as bamboo.

"They won't be for long."

"Fine, I was wondering when you were going to give me my clothes back."

Then for the first time Cassy smiled, really smiled.

Goddamnit, he thought, *she's going to laugh.*

"Would you like to meet some men?"

He stared at her grimly. The question made him uncomfortable. "What is this—a dating agency?"

"I don't understand. Would you like to meet some men...?"

"Always good to see the competition."

Again that strange look. "You are lucky," she said. "It is the time of display."

"Display?" Some kind of fashion show perhaps. He hoped it wasn't bodybuilding; muscles made him queasy.

As they walked, the darkness began to fade into a warm damson glow, and for the first time he could see something that resembled structure, large, three-dimensional portraits each as big as a wall. And in each one...

"My God... Oh God... Oh God!"

Cassy looked at him, her smile thoughtful. "It shocks you? I thought that it might."

"But they're gross..." His stomach heaved. These were not men. Whatever they may have once been ... He stared at Cassy helplessly, the words barely able to form on his lips. "What are they? Why are you showing me this?"

His gaze drifted back to the three nearest cages... or windows; he wasn't sure which. Each housed an individual creature, and then he stepped back to look at them in their entirety. They were vast, lolling frictionless in air that supported them. They reminded him of basking whales, but these were—barely recognisable—men. As he approached, the perfume became even more intense.

A woman slid and fluttered from the velvet shadows, surrounding the display.

"Nycene." Cassy sounded cautious.

"Oh my... what have we here... I mean, I heard but even so." She looked at Peter severely, and then at Cassy. "Has he been treated?"

"No, not yet... but he is perfectly safe... he asked to see the men."

"Curiosity—oh excellent—that is good. I imagine he'll prove playful ... for a time."

Peter stared at them helplessly. This was not as he'd

imagined it. He felt Cassy's hand on his back. She was stroking him.

"Tell him everything," she said.

Peter's gaze remained fixed upon the grotesque mounds of flesh, only half listening to Nycene's explanatory babble.

"Well, of course." She patted Peter's knee. "Whether you see it in terms of art, prestige, or just plain security, men are the ultimate investment. And some women do treat them as investments or even accessories. But *we* know—at least I like to imagine so—these men have emotions! When they are on display, we try to make it special for them, too. The harmonious psyche is everything—a happy man is a happy woman, as they say.

"I like to think of mine–" She pointed to the largest of the three, somnolent, and glowing like varnished chocolate. "Here, Molky—here, boy. *Good* boy." She crooked her little finger and smiled encouragingly as the creature, Molky, slowly opened its eyes and drifted towards the perimeter. Its blank, smiling face stared back at them. "I like to think of Molky as family rather than an investment."

Peter found himself staring at its toenails. She caught his glance and chuckled. "We have the widest range of colours: Penis-Pink, Geldy- Red, Klychie-Glitter, Man-San Silver, Male-Argent, War-Boy Blue. The black ones have the feet for it of course, real tonal contrast."

"Hi, little man! Good boy. Aren't you just so completely delicious?"

Peter recognised the voice and turned to see Niko gliding towards them with reptilian ease. For a moment, he thought she was speaking to him, and he shivered, but she continued her advance past him and reached through the perimeter. Molky squatted and Niko's hand curled round the rolls of fat ringing the man's neck. She kneaded them like bread dough.

Nycene sighed as if regretting something already lost. "He likes you, Niko." She turned to Cassy, "As you see, he's *so* tranquil, clean, well mannered... such a little darling."

Peter was intrigued; he sensed some kind of sales pitch was going on.

Niko smiled, both hands now buried deep in the creature's neck. "He's a credit to you Nycene. I don't know how you do it."

"It really depends on the breed, of course. You can only shape what you're given."

"I think *you* could shape anything, Nycene." Niko's voice had slipped into a husky purr, and Peter felt his penis quiver and die.

"For some it takes longer."

"Meibra usually settles them... although weaning them from it can be a little troublesome."

Nycene pulled a face. "And some never settle."

Peter followed her gaze into eyes that screamed at them in soundless rage. Bloated and pink, apelike, it loomed dangerously close. Peter stepped back. Lips nuzzled his shoulder. He looked down to see Cassy poised on her toes. "It's quite safe, Jonssonpeterjonsson," she whispered. "His eyes are dangerous but they're trapped in flesh. He's safe to stroke."

Niko disentangled herself from Nycene and took Peter's arm, pulling him towards the enclosure. "Stroke him, he really is quite adorable." She guided his hand until it rested on a roll of flesh. It was as soft as peach, as smooth as silk. Peter looked up, staring into eyes that raged at the stick-like creatures encircling him.

Rassun is still a bit of a handful and yes, he needs Meibra." Nycene purred. "But Molky, if you remember, was little better to start with, positively exuded menace, poor little thing, but to see him now... his smile. You just know his soul is blooming."

"Molky will sell at a good price," said Niko.

"And Rassun. It's up to you of course." Nycene pulled herself away and the two women sat facing each other, their eyes interlocked and fathomless. Cassy's arm was wrapped firmly round Peter's hips.

Nycene spoke first. "Molky is happy in himself. He responds to massage. He looks beautiful. He carries his weight with grace. Moccus can have Rassun."

"And him?" asked Cassy.

Peter turned, feeling heavy and, at the same time, very frightened. Cassy's arm remained round his hips, her fingers now fondling his penis now suddenly small. Something exploded within him, an overwhelming urge to break free and run, but his legs felt like water, and his heart pounded in a drum that couldn't move.

Niko approached him cautiously. She looked him straight in the eye as if she owned him. "You will be mine," she said.

Peter exerted every fibre of his body. He wanted to spit and kick, punch the smugness from her face. And all she did was look at him with an air of quiet superiority. Without knowing when, he had become an animal. Something owned, something to be fattened and tamed.

"Put him with the other." She pushed him and he toppled back onto air that suddenly thickened. Cassy accompanied him as he drifted alongside her into an adjoining cage. It was empty except for a large ornately carved jar—Meibra, he guessed. Peter stared at it longingly. He would have to drink. But not yet... not yet.

Cassy poured some into a cup. "Drink, you will need it."

The way she said it frightened him.

"What does it do?"

"It... deadens the mind."

"And?"

"It changes you. Flesh accumulates as you breathe. It doesn't take long. The real problem will be weaning you from it—should we keep you."

Peter shivered. This was real, no dream, nor hallucination... a different dimension? He'd heard about them... people disappeared, and yet he knew that somewhere close, Newport's traffic hummed. His mouth opened to scream; somehow he forced it shut.

He turned instead, facing the adjoining pen. Something, still recognisably a man, stared back at him. His breasts were huge and symmetrical, oiled pendulous boulders resting heavily upon a vast and rounded stomach. His breathing was laboured, making huge ripples of fat as his lungs fought for every mouthful of air.

"Stand." The voice was gentle, yet imperious at the same time. The cage seemed suddenly fragile as the mountain of flesh sighed, then lumbered onto all fours. Arms, creased in overhanging rolls of fat, quivered in exertion. Peter's gaze drifted and stopped at the creature's legs, at knees and feet engulfed in even heavier protrusions of flesh. Then with a groan, a sudden painful gasp, the creature heaved itself up. Peter ached in sympathy.

"Good boy." Cassy gestured, and the man sighed, his body appearing to lighten as the air jellied around him. He stared at them dully, quiet gratitude evident in his gaze. Peter was reminded of a cow he had once fed grass to as a boy.

"He needs this now more than he needs Meibra," she said.

"Horrible." Peter shuddered.

"No. See how comfortable he is. It's about making them feel good." Cassy smiled.

"Feel good." *Yeah, sure.*

"Acceptance brings with it the benign temperament we seek."

"And those who don't—accept?"

"Moccus takes them." Cassy span round at the same time as Niko oozed smoothly from darkness. "If that is your choice."

A sudden bellow shook the jelly-like gloom and the air quivered about them. Peter turned, accepted the Meibra from Cassy's hand and drank it in a single gulp.

They were mountainous, covered in excrement and cushioned on air. In their eyes he saw anger, and fear, dull acceptance—no single expression. Occasionally one panicked, and air vibrated as it shouldered the barriers to either side and bellowed in pain; but with no space, there was little momentum—just the dull, relentless push from those behind.

"These are for Moccus?"

Niko filled his cup with Meibra. "People find his meat addictive."

A vision of rust-coloured shadows filled Peter's mind, jaws on bones and flesh—his flesh. He saw a thin, crimson man, a bristling shadow that grew in size. A grunt reverberated in the darkness. Hunger or laughter.

Martin Brownlow's Cat

Cats have nine lives, a woman has one.

Martin Brownlow was sitting where I was told he would be, holding his beer glass as if it were a stone. He didn't look like a man who enjoyed a drink. He didn't look like a man who enjoyed anything very much, but there he was, sitting where he sat every evening for as long as anyone could remember.

The Hollybush in Tintern was off the main road, some distance from the Abbey itself and favoured by those who knew it. No jukebox or fruit machine; nothing much really at all, except the smell of beer and a sharp haze of tobacco.

I studied him closely before threading my way across an almost empty room. His face had a yellowish tinge, as if it had been carved from candle wax, and he wore a plum-coloured greatcoat that looked as if it had come from the last century—or earlier.

There could be no mistake. I had seen his kind before, shocked off balance, some into madness by their touch with the Otherworld. I wondered where he had come from, and how much he would tell me—though if the rumours were true, I would have little trouble with the latter.

Brownlow had achieved a certain notoriety as Tintern's own ancient mariner, willing to buttonhole anyone who would sit for a moment to listen. Few now gave him the time of day, his story known in rumour and lost in memory. It was generally thought that he was mad, but not dangerous.

"Mind if I sit down?"

He looked at me through watery eyes and placed a hand in one of his pockets, as though searching for tobacco. Then he nodded. In his eyes there was puzzlement, and something else: an overwhelming look of despair that explained at once why most now avoided him. He said nothing, just looked at me, and I wondered whether local rumour was true, or whether for him, too, it was a case of a story now lost in memory.

"I am interested in the Otherworld." And envious, too. There were moments, like these, when I felt like a small boy, face pressed against the windows of something magical. I took a small recorder from my pocket. "I've interviewed—recorded the accounts of many who have been there—or thought they had—"

"I have been there," he said. He looked at the small machine with interest, and I knew I had him.

I pressed the Record, watching the fascination in his face. But he said nothing, and it was I that spoke. "And yet every account I have is different—almost as if, somehow, people slip into an experience that finds them wanting—and each experience is different."

For the first time he smiled but to my disappointment remained silent. For an ancient mariner he was doing a fine job of getting his interrogator to talk. "It may be that we are allowed only into the borders of this Otherworld—it may be that they play with us, or somehow we are judged. I don't know." I found myself shrugging, feeling at once foolish, my finger poised to stop the machine.

"I was found wanting," he said.

"Who are you?" I knew the answer to that. The question was a formality, one for the recorder.

"Martin Brownlow, former preacher, and once a man of God. The two are not always the same," he added.

"But," I hazarded, "a scholar also, I think."

"It was an age of scholars, sir. Ashmole, Hook, Newton—"

"You knew Isaac Newton?"

"Of him." His tone was dismissive as if Newton, too, were somehow to be found wanting. "His friend, John Wickens, took up a living near here at Stoke Edith."

"I've never heard of him."

"He was a good man, sir, though in some way also the author of my present misfortune. It was he who introduced me to the works of Elias Ashmole and others who questioned the nature of our reality. Have you read of his angelical stone, sir?"

I shook my head, noting his disappointment.

"No matter, now," he said.

"What was it, this angelical stone?"

He grimaced, patting his pocket once more. "A stone that lodges in the fires of eternity, granting one converse with angels and—" He broke off, looking at me sharply. "The devil's alchemy, all of it. All of it vanity—avoid its seduction, sir. Vanity, obsession—it taints the soul."

I hazarded another guess. "And yet, I imagine you found the legends surrounding the Devil's Pulpit of some interest—even as a man of God?" I thought then I might have gone too far, but he didn't take offence.

For the first time he smiled, a tight-lipped affair. His eyes flickered towards the window, as if in the darkness beyond he could see the ridge and, upon it, a rough granite slab.

"You know about stones?"

I nodded. "It's a common feature in those who experience the Sidhe."

"Aye, old Elias knew about the Sidhe," he said. "Or thought he did. But let me tell you, sir, the Devil's Pulpit does not allow converse with angels, or transport you to any godly realm."

He glanced up, the brightness of his eye for the moment disguising the darkness beneath. "I was a scholar, a student of antiquities. My most prized possessions were Leland's Itinerary and a book of his notes considered then too rough for publication."

"I know of Leland."

"So you know that he gives a detailed account of the Devil's Pulpit and of those who disappeared in its proximity."

I didn't know that, but nodded. "And did the legends give any indications as to why or how these people disappeared?"

He laughed humourlessly. "Aye, every kind of incantation and pagan devilry. And I tried them all to no avail, until at last, one summer's eve, I slept on it—as sober then as I am now—and there..."

"And there?"

"I dreamt something that was more than a dream."

When he spoke, I had the uncanny sense of listening to one recorder playing back to another.

"I found myself walking down unfamiliar streets." He paused for a moment, his eyes tensed in slits, as if seeking to recall a memory he found painful.

It was night, and the streets were black and narrow. Looming over me on either side were houses, terraced and made from what appeared to be a dull, red marble.

I walked alone, in a dark, soft drizzle, and passed an even narrower lane. There something caught my eye. I stopped, wondering what it was about a black and silver puddle that had caught my attention. Then I saw it again. Movement. A small density of shadow that seemed almost to breathe.

Against all my instincts, but as if I had little choice, I

walked closer and there beheld a cat that died even as I watched. It was a piteous sight, and I would have walked away thinking on the mystery of life and the mercy of our Good Lord, Who holds even the dumbest of creatures in the palm of His hand.

And then I saw movement, but here was no feline Lazarus. Beneath the cooling warmth of its mother, a kitten stirred and pulled itself free as if sensing my presence. At that moment my fate was sealed. I bent and scooped up the damp creature, felt its warmth, the soft rasp of its tongue, and placed it in my pocket.

Now at least I had a companion in this cold, empty world. I proceeded on my way, taking turns at random, but each street seemed to me the same as the last. Black and narrow, and framed by the same dull red terraced buildings that lacked, I now noticed, both windows and doors.

I don't know how long I walked that night, but gradually I became aware of a dragging weight in the pocket that held the kitten. I put in my hand and pulled out, with not a little astonishment, a full-grown cat. It looked at me as demurely as a maid, confident in her ability to charm. Her eyes gleamed like amber in a mask of black velvet. And I knew, don't ask me how, that what I held in my hands was no tom.

Her eyes widened, as if saying to me: I am here. What are you waiting for? And, without really knowing what I was doing, I raised the now purring creature to my neck and chin, taking strength from its warmth.

I wondered whether it would flee, should I put it down, but the creature made the decision for me, clambering onto my shoulder where it nestled, purring its approval into my ear.

I have never seen a city so vast or strange or silent, and every house and every street the same, so that it seemed that I was walking but the one street time over time. And with each step, the creature seemed to grow in substance, its paws heavy, its claws digging into the fabric of my coat. I could feel its weight, firm against my back, dragging slightly, swaying as I walked.

'Martin.'

The voice was directly in my ear, and as I turned, I became aware of a pale white arm, amber eyes staring into my own, and then a sudden release of weight. A woman walked the street beside me. For the briefest of moments, I had a sense of sinful nakedness, her slenderness barely clothed by a flow of raven hair extending to her waist and thighs. And then the moment was gone and a woman, both modest and sober, stood by my side. Her dress was of the dark blue of midnight; her raven hair now held in check by a white linen cap.

She looked at me from amber eyes, her voice a soft purr rising to a tone as pure as a bell. 'Martin,' she said. 'Do I please you?'

When I awoke, she was bending over me, her breath warm and sweet as honey.

'I caused you to faint,' she said.

I knew then I was in the Devil's hands, this creature sent to tempt me. And yet I saw her eyes glisten, as if my evident revulsion caused her sorrow.

'What you see, I will be.'

I remember shaking my head. 'I saw a cat.'

Her small chin set in determination. She leant down, staring into my face. 'I love, therefore, I am,' she said, her voice grave and sweet. 'It is our nature to be what we love.'

I started up from the ground, rising unsteadily to my feet. The red and black terrain of the night had gone, and we were alone in empty countryside, the day yet fresh. 'What manner of world is this?' I said, as if blaming her for my present misfortune.

'It is my world, and everything here is as you would want.'

I shut my eyes, holding my head firmly between both hands. Was I wishing *her*, and thus succumbing to the wiles of Satan—or was she wishing me into her own damnation? I screwed my eyes tighter, remembering the small ball of fur in my pocket, willing her back. When I opened my eyes she was still there, regarding me gravely.

'I cannot love you truly in the form that you found me,' she said. 'Come. Many stay, and your mind may change.'

She took my hand in hers, and I felt the warmth of her body and the sweetness of her breath, and I wanted her so much. But the Lord gave me strength, and we walked the very road that Bunyan tells of, traversing hell and paradise.

We took a dreary road, shaded on either side by trees, their roots and branches encroaching so much on the path, it was like walking through a bleak and terrible tunnel. I confess that I was then glad to have the woman on my arm, for she walked with confidence and not a shred of fear—as if it were I that gave *her* strength.

We came at last to a gnarled oak against which a man in good attire was casually leaning. He raised his hat to my companion, who smiled as if she knew him, and together the three of us fell in side by side. I waited but a moment, expecting either him or the woman to make what introductions were necessary, but none was forthcoming. Before I could open my mouth, the path spread out onto a bare apron of land; beyond was a great mountain cloaked in forest. The sun was already low; the sky, a livid red against which great conifers loomed like black, ferocious torches.

At once the stranger turned round, addressing me directly. 'You have something that belongs to me.'

I felt the woman pressing into me, felt her warmth. Her grip on me tightened.

'He loves me,' she said, her voice as soft as cream. And at that moment I did, consumed as I was by a terrible lust. I saw the stranger smile at me.

'Martin Brownlow,' he said. 'I repeat, you have something of mine, and yet I see you hesitate.'

At that moment I knew who my adversary was, and at the same time marvelled at my own composure. With a strength that comes when heaven is watching, I disentangled myself from the creature that had so strangely excited me. I pushed her away, avoiding her eyes for the pain I knew I would see there.

'I will not brook unnatural entanglements. Man is born with an immortal soul. I will not conjoin with an animal.' I heard then a sudden, sharp cry of pain, and at the same time the stranger hissed, like one suppressing a great and terrible anger.

That cry, it haunts me still. I turned my back, tried to avoid the woman's eyes, the hurt, and yes, the tenderness I knew I would find there. Yet, to my eternal shame, I felt a horrible gladness when I sensed her presence behind me, her hand on my shoulder. I breathed in deeply, hoping for a trace of her scent.

'I love you, Martin,' she said. 'I am what you have always hoped for. Is that not true?' She sounded bewildered.

I groaned and shook her off, and looked directly into the eyes of my adversary.

His words flowed then as free as weeds, each one rooting, clouding my mind.

'You would destroy me,' I said at last, 'break me apart. For a man who is not friends with God is no longer a friend to himself.'

He regarded me quizzically and raised his hand, running fingers through his long, dry hair. 'Aye, but then again, if you're friends with yourself, then surely all is right with your God,' he said.

'The happy sinner—'tis the Devil's casuistry.' I don't to this day know where such boldness came from, to argue thus with the Lord of Darkness. But the stranger appeared to take no offence; instead, smiling broadly, he laid a familiar arm across the woman's shoulder.

'Ah, but preferable to the *unhappy* sinner. As to my nature, I fear you do misjudge me, Martin.'

He stood there before me, as proud as any eastern potentate, and I watched him kiss the girl gently on the lips. What confusion of thoughts whirled within me at that moment? Jealousy and anger jostled in my bosom, and he laughed scornfully in my face.

He claimed possession of her, but whether as a king or father, or one who would be her suitor, I could not tell. He was holding her hand, talking to me.

'You know nothing of this world, and yet you judge. You would break a heart for your God.'

He looked up into the sky, as if sensing things I couldn't see. And then I, too, heard what sounded first like faint birdsong. As I listened, the sound became clearer, turning into a bewildering confusion of voices you might have heard on a London street. At once the stranger left us, rushing into the clearing like a sinister crow, and about him forms materialised in a blaze of black and orange light.

They emerged from nowhere, these imps from hell, and smiles of welcome gleamed darkly as each in turn paused to look upon us. Music swirled like an invisible fog, becoming ever more rhythmic and wild. The effect was startling and immediate, for man, woman, and child began a leaping and a shrieking, as if the very devil had them by the heels, and well he might and so it did appear.

They twirled and tumbled in intricate circles, their dance becoming more heated, more frenzied as the music wailed and throbbed. And the air thickened in lust, the music becoming ever darker. In twos and fours they fell about me, coupling feverishly like rats on heat.

And I saw the effect on the woman beside me. She was shivering, holding my hand, pulling, and all the time my adversary, master of this devilish community, was staring at her, his eyes as wide as the circles of hell.

'See how she struggles to join them, Martin.'

'And yet she resists your wiles.' I turned to her then, proud in her strength. 'Come with me, back to my world.' I didn't then know what I was saying.

'Back to your world, you say; but what world is that?'

I tried to tell him, in every way I could, that I wanted to go back, but the stranger laughed.

'Go back to where?'

He told me then of all those who had preceded me, and all those yet to come until my very head rang, and I found myself crying, the woman's arms holding me, her breath in my ear.

'I will go back with you,' she said, and a strange combination of lust and dread took possession of me. I held her hand, aware that all were looking at us with their pale cat-like eyes.

The stranger took her from me, looking gently into her face. 'If that is your will, but you will sing for your freedom—after you have been reminded of a world you will not find again.' His voice had softened, and I sensed for the first time a great and hidden tenderness.

He raised his hands to a sky now dark, and the dancing stopped, the music died. And there came upon us a whisper that swelled into something soulless and vile: the irascible rustle of leaves and reeds; the howling of unknown beasts, and savages destined for hell; a great wind, lost and wailing in high mountain peaks; the shriek of a fox—or a baby crying.

I was hearing the sound of a wilderness given tongue. And as I listened, the sounds seemed to merge, forming a strain of dark solemnity in which I heard the voices of martyred friends, the pleadings of my long-dead wife, the children I would never have. It was, my friend, the music of fiends tearing away the final shreds of sense and rational thought.

And then it was her turn to sing, and I heard a voice so pure I knew then she was no devil, no succubus, no instrument sent for my damnation, but when I looked at her, all I saw was the cat underneath.

That same foul mix of lust and despair overcame me as the woman, sensing her victory, edged closer. If she had touched me then, I knew I would have been forever lost.

'Can it be that you are changed so utterly?' I spoke in hope and wonder. 'But if that then is the case, what reality is there to our being?'

'What you see, believe in,' she said. 'Please, Martin.'

His chant was soft, in a tongue unknown to Christian man. He took from his pocket a cloth of black silk and he polished the air about him as though it were a mirror. And thereupon I saw a soft glow increasing in intensity until we were immersed in a shower of light.

'Go now, the two of you—if that is your choice.' There was pain in his voice, as if even now he would have taken her from me.

I took one last look at the woman standing proudly by my side; saw for the last time her human terror—the love that remained in her eyes.

I stopped the tape. "What happened to her? Did she not come with you?"

He put down his glass, and from his pocket he took out

a small black cat with amber eyes. It looked at me as demurely as a maid, confident in her ability to charm.

Housebound

There is such a house... somewhere in Newport.

I can't remember how I found the house. That in itself is part of the problem, one I've retraced many times in my mind, until it has become more than an obsession. It has become my entire life. And worse, I cannot now remember how to leave it. You think my mind wanders perhaps—like a child's—and yes, there have been times I have run through these rooms like a child, searching for the tiniest crevice or crack through which I might slip out.

The book lies upon the desk. In it are glimpses of who I was, and what I have done, and they vanish as I turn the page.

Sometimes I wake up, still warm in dream. I am walking up Stow Hill and before reaching its brow I take a left and then turn right. Within moments I am lost in a warren of old houses that seem to multiply even as I walk. And the faster I walk the more numerous become the streets, each twisting off at sly angles, until at last the house appears, as if by magic. That was how it was the first day.

The house I remember, always the house. It hangs like a large landscape, a painting by Hopper, and I see it whenever I close my eyes.

It is set on the edge of a small graveyard, and is tall, and of a pale, sickly blue as if it has been soaked in twilight. It reminded me of a vast mausoleum, neither gothic nor classical but shifting between the two, depending from which angle you regarded it, or even perhaps your state of mind.

And yet the house in itself was not unusual. I had seen many similar in Newport, built during the Regency period for aspiring merchants with Palladian pretensions. Even the small graveyard may have been less than it looked: a folly perhaps, with its ivy streaked marbles, porticos and domes.

Nor was the house in any way sinister, at least on the outside. It still retained an air of faded grandeur, its steps worn though free from debris or leaves, railings black, shiny as if newly painted, and there was a comforting dry smell to the door. I can put it no better than that.

Yes, I remember the house, my dear Anne, but not always your face, for it always changes. And yet you stay in my mind, and I know you are waiting for me. That is something I have to imagine, or else I would go mad. Some weeks ago—it may have been months, even longer—I dreamt of you and woke up with a start, grabbing pencil and paper and scrawling down these few lines:

Bubbly, mousy hair, slightly tremulous lips and blue, watery eyes, her face reminded him of a raindrop, and he loved her.

You see it helps, seeing you through the eyes of another; it makes you more stable, for my own memory has become frail. Once, I was able to rehearse whole conversations with you, until gradually your voice became fainter, evaporating like an echo that has grown tired of itself.

Why can I remember this building, in all its exotic, shifting detail, and yet depend on this third person scrawl to recapture your memory, precious, but possibly false?

And yet I remember the arguments, some of them, those I've written down. I have a hundred different versions of, and not all of them can be true, not entirely so, for they change and contradict each other so that sometimes I feel that I'm arguing against a hundred of you, all with a different face.

'It's either the house or me,' delivered in a petulant whine. It's a cliché, which is why I think Anne may have said it. I'm staring at the line now. It's underlined, and there's an arrow leading to other phrases: 'It's destroying you—can't you see that?' 'It's taking from you more than you have.'

And now I remember.

"I give it blood." I wave my scarred arms across her face, open my shirt.

She looks at me scornfully. "And after that? Can't you see where your mind is taking you? You are mortgaging your soul to a nightmare. Obsessions are never satisfied—even with blood."

I tell her what the house really means to me. I tell her my secret.

Her face changes and she shakes her head slowly as the enormity sinks in.

"The house is built upon temporal sands," I tell her, "offering a thousand different paths to a thousand other worlds. And yes, there's a price to be paid." Again I thrust my arm towards her. There's pity in her face as she scans the blood-pattern of weal and scab extending up to my shoulders and neck.

"Temporal sands... that's rubbish." Then she looks at me—uses her softest voice. "You'll lose your mind in time."

I laugh at that, and she thinks I'm laughing at her.

She looks around the shadowy hallway, and now her voice is angry. "Temporal sands—sounds like a bloody sea resort, a Farrow and Ball colour chart. And you, you're painting yourself in with illusion."

I laugh again. I'm laughing now.

"And before you know it, you'll be trapped—then see if I care!" She strides towards the door, a small suitcase in her hand. She turns—one final riposte. "This isn't a house. It's a bloody mausoleum." The door slams shut behind her.

I write this down, before I forget. It joins a jigsaw of arguments that twist and turn, never entirely makes sense except in this: the house values me and does not value Anne. And now she is gone.

Sometimes I feel as if the house has become part of me, that it sees through my eyes, guides me—on occasions comforts me. Sometimes it is stern. I remember the noise as the door first shut behind me, a long low sigh—as if somehow the house knew I was there and was accepting me with considered reluctance.

The thought that the sigh might have been one of anticipation came later. Whatever the case, the house seemed to breath around me, and as I stepped further in—passing quickly through the hall with its harlequin patterned tiles. Shadows gathered as if in welcome, and footsteps slipped by, leading me into new rooms, leading me further and further into its depths.

It felt as though I were pushing my way through something almost gelatinous, stumbling through a thousand presences, an invisible crowd, their whispering almost too soft to hear. They seemed to be guiding me, and I drifted where their unseen jostling led. Within moments I was drawn to the entrance of a small and rather shabby room.

When I close my eyes the room comes vividly to life, so that I feel I could step into it without leaving my desk. It has a rough wooden floor lined with dust. In the centre of the room is a red and blue Persian rug. It lies alongside what appears to be a trapdoor that I guessed lead down to a cellar.

As I walked into the room, the whispering around me intensified, falling silent as I approached the cellar door. They wanted me to go down, but I knew I wouldn't. Not yet. Instead I positioned myself near the rug, shifting it with my foot until it covered the trapdoor. In doing so it became apparent that the rug had previously hidden something else, a dark irregular stain that might have been dried blood. And then the jostling resumed and I found myself being pushed from apartment to apartment, until at last I came to where I now write.

It is a small study, and I walked across it, tracing my fingers along the paneling, like some kind of aberrant cat, making it his own. The window was large and opened wide and I walked out into a large, stone courtyard that led into a rank and verdant wilderness.

The yard was paved and given shape by a series of worn pillars furred in lichen, sleek and virulently green. In the middle of the court was an ancient fountain, dominated by a large and vapid looking cherub. When twilight fell, these most mundane of materials slowly arranged themselves into sinister patterns, and every night I made sure to lock the window tight.

On that first day however the day was bright, a low autumnal sun bathing the greenery in a warm, golden light. Around the perimeter, tall trees provided a dark, ragged frame, which gave a degree of privacy to the lunatic garden with its domes and headstones, crosses, its marbled mock crypts.

From the garden the house looked as if it were slowly sinking into the earth. A large ash tree had already breached the low stonewall separating patio from natural wilderness, its rippling shade an active challenge, a warning of what would follow. A small breeze took up, making me shiver, and about my feet woodlice scuttled across the cobbles like tiny surfers catching the wave, rounding stone after stone before disappearing where the shade was most deep.

I returned to the house, to the room I saw now as my own. I remember feeling then content.

I had bought the house unseen in a London auction. Anne had been typically sniffy about the whole thing, refused to accept its knockdown price, its potential as investment property, the fact that I knew Newport well, and that its fortunes were on the up. It took two bottles of champagne before she was sufficiently mollified to mutter something about at least not having bought it on EBay.

I gaze down at the page, and turn it over. I wonder how long the memory will remain. Like everything else, recollection comes and goes, and that is how it is for me: the house has taken over; outside has lost its meaning. It is why I write, to set things down, capture the elusive. Sometimes I think the house is sucking at my mind, absorbing what I am, what I was, and when I am dead only this book will remain.

In one of the rooms there is small library of slim volumes bound in red leather; very similar to the one I am writing in now. On occasions a morbid fancy grips me—that they record the struggle of past unfortunates who sought to escape, thus holding on to their memories, their souls. There are two reasons why I have not put the theory to the test: the room is never in the same place twice, and on the few occasions I have found myself in it, I've been too afraid to try.

As well as this journal, I still have the letters I know I won't post, but I read them to you, Anne. Every night I read them to you. And once, just once you came to visit me.

And that was it.

I remember your face now. You look concerned and you're telling me to see someone, and yes, I love you, so I will see someone, but we quarrel, and you hurt me, and now I'm alone, haunting a house that loves me, *really* loves me.

Occasionally the house sets me tasks, usually in the form of dreams. When I awake I remember them as such but later, when I come to write them down or read them back to myself—and sometimes to you, Anne—I'm never quite sure how to separate the dream from my day.

I give you an example. There is a library in the house, in fact there are several, although the larger library is one of my favourites.

It is a room of tables, black in dust or age. On them are books, strewn across every surface as if they were doubloons. Most are bound in pale leather, some inscribed with small patterned diamonds of emerald or red; they gleam briefly as my torch passes over them.

On other tables are parchments, dry and curled like large autumnal leaves waiting for a wind that will never blow. There are folios there, too, exotic quills, and quartos bound in subtle skins. At the far end of the library two corridors branch out on either side and each leads on to two smaller rooms, one of which has an Egyptian air to it, or at least that of a tomb. It is filled with shards of ancient pottery and in the shadows, arranged on chairs, a small number of sinister looking mummies stare back at me. They are leathery and crudely bound, but their faces have been brightly painted.

The other room is almost bare, except for a picture and a thin window that opens out on the lawn and offers views beyond. The picture is in the corner. At first I thought it was you, but it isn't. I took out my paper and checked. Maybe someone else once lived here and drew what he remembered of his wife, or his daughter... a girl friend perhaps.

The picture is of someone special. There are candles around it—unlit—and a small golden lamp above with a faint trace of unguents and spice. Overlaying this hint of incense is the heavier, more familiar odour of vellum and wax, the must of decaying parchment.

At first, the whisper was soft, but gradually it became louder, buzzing around my head like a large and oily fly. The house was insistent. I was to transfer every fragment of flesh and clay from one room to another, arranging each one according to its period, function and condition.

How many days—weeks—months did I spend, patiently transferring these urns and shards, the feather-light bodies that threatened to crumble in my arms as I walked with them from room to room? I have no way of telling. Only that I did it diligently and, as my dream dictated, carrying the fragments in my teeth. And nor do I think it was entirely dream, for every morning I awoke tired, my mouth filled with crumbs of dry clay that tasted of cake.

Sometimes, it made me sick. I remember once staggering from the couch, my throat dry and tight as though, during the night I had swallowed a series of small bricks. I tried to cough them out, and then swallow them but the effort only made things worse and I barely made the bathroom in time. My face was green in the mirror and when I pulled my head back, wall, mirror and basin moved up as well, fixing themselves briefly to the ceiling before juddering down in time to receive a further load of spew. I clung on to the rim of the basin, holding it down, holding myself up.

The air was rarely fresh in the house and an odour of vomit lingered about me. I wanted to feel rain on my face and so it came upon me that now would be a good time to bury your ring.

In the garden, the smell of wet grass and mint hits you at once. The grass is high and perpetually damp, and however far or fast you run you always come back to where you started. I walked across to the rampant ash tree, carefully stepping over the ruined wall. There, where the garden began, I knelt down and started to dig among the dead leaves, sinking my fingers into mildew and earth. A light rain was falling and my back and shoulders became heavy in damp. It was where I knew it would be, the moist soil covering it like a crumbling blanket. I held it up, brushing off earth, watching it flake like inky snow between my knees.

The box rattled slightly as I prised open the lid. Inside were ten or twelve rings, a few fragments of bone. There I placed your ring, Anne, safe for when you may need it. And then I stared for a moment at those other rings, wondering where they had come from, and who had put them there. The thought bothered me, and after I had placed the box back into the ground, I positioned myself on one of the larger roots and tried to puzzle it out. Who did these other rings belong to, and how had I known where to bury Anne's ring?

I thought again of that small library of slim volumes bound in red leather, and my earlier fancy that each of them might, too, record the sacrifices of those who had previously lived here. I walked reluctantly back over the wall, back into the house. I was feeling sick again, my mind a whirl of conflicting thoughts. Why had Anne left me like this, and how many others had been sacrificed to the house?

The afternoon had been sticky, the evening was hot, sultry with cloud that thickened and massed over a jumble of brick and slate. The wind was picking up and in the narrow street below I could hear the faint scraping of leaves, jostling for position in dry, random scurries. I stared out from the window, tracing the sky from the lit Transporter Bridge, where the clouds were thickest, skimming over chimneys and roofs, and marked out the city, landmark by landmark: the pale green dome of the old art college, the office block, below that the castle. The excitement was physical. My hands pressed down upon the window ledge, but still they trembled. The house would unleash me tonight, it surely would.

The wind grew stronger, the night more dark, and a fierce volley of sleet swept the empty streets, turning greyness into lakes of silver and black. It was turning into a night where ghouls might walk, and stories told of wrecks and goblins, where old men sat by fires. It is easy to write such things, trapped in a house such as this.

Above me I heard the chimneys rumbling, the windows rain-smeared and stammering to each gust of wind. Occasionally the walls shook as if grasped by invisible giants. Yes definitely tonight.

When the elements are so unsettled, I like to imagine the house loses some of its power over me, but deep inside I know the truth. I am released because it knows I will return. Like something tamed.

The air was static, prickling my skin. Away from the window, the night outside was flat like glass, as black as ink. I put on my shoes slowly, anticipating the door closing behind me, the street outside, and I remembered all those times I had tried to break out on my terms, with no strings attached.

But this house has my measure. At first I thought it enjoyed my misery, observing with quiet malice my early attempts at escape. Some of them were finely planned, others spontaneous and desperate, hoping to succeed through luck or surprise. And every time a door was not where it should have been, or vanished as I approached; the windows proved immovable, unbreakable. People walked by as if the house were somehow invisible, and however many times I howled or hammered on what appeared to be fragile glass, the result remained the same. I might as well have not existed. The house had me like a fly in a bottle.

It was a relationship... a House... Fly, both of us dependent on the other, as one in our need.

And with realization had come release.

I looked down at my shoes, brown and brightly polished, both tightly laced. And then I straightened, hurled myself across the room. I raced down stairs that held their shape, hurtled across the harlequin patterned hall, and wrenched the door open before it disappeared.

I was in the street and couldn't believe it. The storm had temporarily abated, and I paused briefly to gather my breath, sheltering beneath the narrow porch. The air was wet and fresh, and water dripped in translucent pearls of light. I could have cried.

There was a soft sigh behind me and with it the feeling that, if I stayed just a moment longer, the house in the form of an affectionate but distracted mother would scoop me up in her hands and whisk me back inside. I leapt down the steps, tearing through the narrow maze of streets, instinctively heading downhill, always downhill. Time blipped and a moment later, or so it seemed, I was panting like a winded horse, crouched within the shadows of a large, imposing bank.

Newport seemed empty, its pubs, glimpsed through steamed up windows, only half full, its central street a rain-swept gully. There were trees there, gaunt and skeletal, each caught in their own frozen wail. One end of the street led to the docks, the other to the castle, fragments of country and roads leading elsewhere.

I turned down a side street that I knew would take me to the river, and eventually the bridge. The rain was pouring down, splashing off huddled cars, overflowing gutters, turning the twisty streets into even more of a wasteland.

I could have sheltered under the castle underpass but the shadows frightened me, and I ran lightly through it and up the steps that led to the bridge.

The bridge was made of stone and baldly lit. The river was dark, making a rushing noise underneath. On the other side were takeaways, seedy looking shops, and from somewhere there came the sound of drums, a hoarse voice and a louder guitar.

The road released me into a small square, and I found myself stumbling into what to do next. Which way to go? Then I saw her, across the road, sheltering in the shadows of an abandoned cinema.

Slow down... slow down. I slipped into a shop-doorway. Its windows were dusty. The one to my left belonged to a fancy dress outlet, the other sold homebrew equipment. I shifted my gaze back to the girl, examining her from head to toe. She was perfect—seventeen, maybe eighteen. Her hair was arranged in loose ringlets, its darkness bringing out a pale face. Perhaps too pale—nothing that a touch of paint wouldn't bring out. She was dressed in black and held a pink umbrella. She looked bored and wet. Every now and again she would look up at the sky, as though assessing the strength of the rain. Once she looked at her watch.

Then she moved. She was quick. I almost missed her. She walked briskly and I wanted to hold her, imagined my arm about her waist, that over-pale face turning round in fear and eventual acceptance. I wondered about her nails, those colourless lips. She would come up nice, painted. The street was long and her umbrella was angled, pushing against rain and wind. I focused on her hips, the gentle sway of her bum. Just for a moment, I closed my eyes, enjoying the dark swish of the rain, the clicking of her heels.

The clicking stopped. I opened my eyes barely in time. She was standing in front of a large red-bricked house and staring up at a lit bedroom. Even from where I stood, I could see she was smiling. An older version of herself was waving down at her. I guessed it was her mother and watched as she pushed open the sash window.

"I'll be back before midnight, mum." Her voice was as thin as cotton and wavered in the gusty wind.

"Where's Terry?"

"He's waiting for me in the pub—I should have been there by now."

"He'll wait. I'll expect you at midnight then—don't make it much later."

Don't make it much later. I smile at that, lost in the memory.

The mother smiles to and closes the curtain. I notice she's left the window open. Strange, I think, on a night like this. I wait a moment longer, then catch up with the girl. We are the only people on the street. She may have heard my footsteps, but she doesn't turn; her pace increases; pretty soon she's running.

We are coming up to a small junction. Across the road is a narrow alley, and beyond that, wasteland, tawny in the urban light and mottled in shadow.

It has to be now.

But I am too late, my reactions slow. A man appears. Terry. He's holding the woman tight, guiding her, pushing her across the road, and she's laughing, pressing herself against him, stealing his warmth.

I stare at the page blankly, seeing what happened next as from a distance.

I followed them, watch as they vanish into a pub. The bar was crimson lit and wavered in drifting clouds of smoke. Steamy shapes moved as if part of a dream denied to me. There was no way in. But I knew where she lived. I knew that, and I knew she'd have a smile on her face after I'd finished.

I turned away, the ruby glow of the inn bleeding like wet paint in the blackness and rain. I was alone in that night, free, but with nowhere to go but home empty handed.

It was after this, my brief and bloodless hunt that the nature of my dreams changed, the house was more unfriendly. It wanted the girl.

I was in the library again, with a newly given and far more formidable challenge and fought to control my breathing, as the immensity and scale of the task became apparent. The transfer and cataloguing of urns and withered flesh, the shards of broken pottery had been only the first of my labours: a test perhaps of my willingness, my endurance. The house was willful; laying before me the full measure of how it would crush me, reduce me in time to a blind and mindless mite.

I stared through the dim kaleidoscope of leather and paper: the jeweled spines, some gold embossed arranged at random across vast tables, the layers of manuscripts, small islands of folios, quartos and hide-bound magazines. And this was only the tiniest fragment of my task. Whole walls were lined with cabinets, covered by dark mahogany bookcases polished to a deep and glossy red. On one wall were shelves that almost touched the ceiling and as I looked I noticed their depth, the strong shadows which separated each of their sections. There were passages between and behind them, a maze I was too frightened to explore. I was suffocating in books.

Not for me the comfort of deep leather chairs, warm fires and ticking clocks. The house was speaking to me, its malice and contempt cold and undisguised. I had not brought *her* back. I explained, a thousand times I explained, how close I had been, how I knew where she lived and how I never failed twice but it wasn't enough. I knew that; nothing would ever be enough for this house. Its message was simple and clear. If I couldn't provide, it would find someone who could. In the meantime it would bury me in mindless tasks, and this was but the first: to read and absorb, to catalogue each and every book, magazine and parchment until my eyesight failed, my mind broke and my body reduced to a dry and yellow dust.

My time now is spent in feverish activity. Some nights are better than others and I exult in the dead wisdom that surrounds me. On nights like these my hands race over the endless books like curious white spiders touching, pausing, now lifting up one volume, discarding, and then another, and so fast, so urgent is my inquiry I feel as though I am being bombarded with books, drowning in knowledge I would never absorb.

At other times I cry.

Whole nights pass and I spend them slumped before a solitary candle staring into its brightness until my eyes hurt and I can see nothing else. Sometimes the house leaves me alone. At other times it shows its impatience, the whispering evermore insistent. I know that there is one more thing I have to do. At the same time I hesitate, whether from reluctance, perhaps even fear, or because I know it is the last thing I might ever do, and I am hoarding it like a miser and his gold.

The house senses this, and finally it relents. *You will not fail me again.*

There is thunder in the air and the air is hot, too thick to breathe. I remember the open sash window and imagine her smile... when it is done.

In the meantime... the house is adamant, its whispers deafening; finish what you have in the cellar. Then bring the girl.

The room is lit, its rough wooden floor skimmed with dust, and below that is a darker stain, like that of dried blood. There is a red and blue rug nearby, and I wonder whether it may have once covered the stain and, if so, who had moved it. I walk cautiously into the centre of the room, creating small flurries the light, dancing like small flies about my feet.

Walls and corners are soft and indistinct, fading into the fine wavering grey of spider-webs. The rug is sharp in focus. I move it to one side and open the trapdoor beneath. A sweet reek of decay lies heavy in the air.

The chill eats into me at once, corrosive like bleach. I am not so much walking as gliding, down into an impenetrable darkness. The torch, a thin and sickly light, illuminates little more than my feet, the occasional patch of grey. I assume they are stairs though they seem only tenuously connected to where I am going.

I picture the darkness seeping up from the soil, and I tighten my grip on the torch, as though somehow I might squeeze out more light.

The cellar is familiar, its walls richly patterned in fungus and rot. A light hangs from the ceiling and it drifts a little from side to side as if moved by an unseen, unfelt breeze. The light dims and flickers, casting a sallow, intermittent glare over the wavering space. Dark patterned walls fade and bleach, along with a sense of what I am doing here.

It's only gradually I realise I am not alone. Someone else is in the room. As I walk closer I see it is a woman, but her face is in shadow and so is everything around her. The room is growing smaller, closing in, watching.

She sits stiffly. The chair may have once been covered in brightly coloured fabric; now it is grimy; yellow foam pokes out where moths have preyed. She is tightly bound in linen. On a table besides her are a small paint box and a smooth vellum mask. There are more masks scattered across the floor.

I study what remains of the face, try to remember her ... bubbly, mousy hair, slightly tremulous lips and blue, watery eyes. I begin to paint. Her face reminds me of a raindrop and I know I love her. I love each and every one of them, but her most of all.

Beside The Seaside, Beside The Sea

Where sky and sea meet there is a line below the horizon.

I found him at the farthest end of the Murenger. He was sitting alone, a table to himself, as though he carried about him a scent of something unpleasant. The thought had come suddenly, and at the same time he lifted his head, as though he had just then read my mind.

"Jack." I extended an arm, which he ignored.

"Andrew," he said. "So you've come."

There was a moment's awkward silence, as I eased myself into the one vacant chair, raised the glass to my lips for the first, preliminary sip. What those around us may have intuitively surmised became evident, as I looked at him over the rim. I tried to make my eyes smile and failed. Jack was dying.

He wore a brown wool cap, the gap above and around his ears hinting at the baldness beneath. A beard that had once been wiry and of a virulent red, was now thin and grey, its shade only a little darker than that of his face. But it was the eyes that frightened me most of all, and yet for no apparent reason. There was nothing monstrous about them, but they seemed strangely sunken, and around them the flesh had darkened as though the pupils were leaking and staining the skin the colour of weak tea.

"Well, have you had a good look?" The eyes glittered like cold marbles as he spoke.

"Yes, Jack. "You're dying, I think."

For the first time he smiled. "Direct answers come from strong souls."

It seemed a strange thing to say, so I just smiled in return and raised the glass once more to my lips. I hadn't seen Jack for at least ten years, not since I had left Liverpool for good. In those golden years Jack had been both physicist and poet, holding court in the snug of the Philharmonic, The Crack,— occasionally The Grapes. Bands had groupies, Jack attracted acolytes, usually with the same end result. What had happened to him, and why was our meeting so urgent?

"A strong soul," he repeated. "Treasure it."

"What has happened to you, Jack? What are you doing here in the Murenger?"

"I have lost something. I want you to find it." He took the glass from my hand, placed it gently on the table, and all the time kept his terrible eyes fixed upon mine. "I remember, in Liverpool, you were up for most things."

"I was young then."

"And are you scared now?"

"Cautious. What is it, Jack? What have you lost ... where do you want me to go?"

He raised his left hand and extended a finger. "I need you to retrieve something. A ring."

I looked at him curiously, wondering why this was not something he could do for himself. "Where did you lose it?"

"Somewhere close but a different dimension." He stared into my eyes, as though daring me to laugh.

I didn't laugh. Instead I said, "So, a rail-card's no good then."

He shrugged, tracing his finger across the rim of his glass and staring into what remained of his beer. "I've done well for myself ... before this happened."

"I know. I've read your book—'*Quantum Magic*'?"

"That's one. I've written several ... but how to explain ... " He stopped and withdrew from his pocket a half bottle of scotch. It was almost empty, and he poured what was left of it into his glass. I could tell by his tone, and what he said next that he was already more than drunk.

"When I was a student, Andrew, I would often go to the beach at night and just stand there, staring at where the sky and sea meet. It's a thin, dark line."

"The horizon."

"Not the horizon. After a while you begin to see things. Strange shapes emerge from the blackness and in your mind you see them coming towards you. I gave them a name—Greylings—little realising that they were calling me and not the other way round."

"Jack," I said gently. "I don't understand."

"You will, Andrew, you will. You see, in this world, you may see it as a fancy, a line drawn in the mind. And yet what if we are sensing what really exists—somewhere else?"

"In another dimension." I was clutching at straws, at the same time wondering whether I would have to take Jack back home with me that night.

Jack drank quickly, and then nodded. "That line between sea and sky hides other worlds,—at least where you are going it does." He shuddered. "I didn't use to, but now I fear the sea. It's the devil's domain, a place of darkness and change, an abyss, where the leviathan lurks, where demons sport. It is from these dark waters that the beast will come." I was conscious that I was smiling. Jack the wordsmith, manipulating, playing with—but slurring—his words.

"You have been to this other place?"

"It is where I lost the ring."

"So, why can't *you* go back and get it? I don't see why you need me."

"A second time would mean my death or worse."

I must have looked unconvinced, because he continued.

"It's a dominion darker than faery, neither demonic nor mortal, heaven nor earth, and yet intimately linked to each." He sighed, and then raised his head, looking me in the eye. "The church was closer than it thought when it created limbo, but where you are going is nowhere near as pleasant. You will be entering a realm of dead souls."

"Souls don't die, Jack. That's the whole point. Souls don't die."

At that he gave me such a look. "A soul can be drained."

The tone, more than the words, caused me to shiver. "You really know how to sell a deal, Jack. What makes you think I'm going to buy into this?"

He chuckled. "Because you're humouring me. Part of you thinks I'm drunk and talking nonsense." He put a hand into his pocket. "And because *by* indulging me, you will come out of it a very rich man."

I examined the cheque he slipped into my hand. "You *do* know how to sell a deal, Jack." I regarded him curiously. "And how do I pass through into this hidden realm. I mean, what are you suggesting—potions—lotions? Do I recant, incant, daub stones in blood, make deals with Old Nick? What is it, Jack? What do you want me to do?"

"You sound like Dylan," he said. "What you have to do is precisely nothing. Where you have to be, is what you need to be asking."

I looked at him; said nothing.

"Planes of reality fold in on themselves, dimensions

overlap, Andrew. Sometimes there are fault lines. Newport is built on one."

I glanced round nervously almost convinced, as much by his expression as by the professorial tone. "Is that good?"

"People can disappear." He sounded amused.

I grimaced. "What about re-appearing?"

"I came back." He read my thoughts, smiled grimly. "And no, the experience will not reduce you to this." His hand reached up to stroke his deeply lined face, and then withdrew, as though his skin no longer belonged to him. It was a horrible moment and the image, the look in his eyes... I shivered and almost involuntarily my hand went up to my own cheeks.

"What happened to you, Jack?" I whispered.

"I left something behind." He raised the ring-less finger. "It must be acting as some kind of conduit." He hugged himself—feebly—as though suddenly cold, and smiled through teeth that were grey. "I'm being drained—and I don't want to go back there, Andrew."

"Where shall we meet," I said.

I checked my watch. If Jack was right, I'd be gone within the minute and back shortly after. The cheque was in my pocket and I looked forward to the morning. Newport docks stood before me, drab, eerie and quietly busy even at night. Jack had positioned me exactly, had been vehement in his warning. I was not to move—even by an inch. Whatever happened I was not to move. He had even chalked round my feet, indicating exactly where I should stand.

About twenty feet or so to my left, the coals of a brazier glowed a vibrant red, and casting an orange tint on a merchant ship anchored alongside. There were voices. I heard a woman laugh. Further down the river, to my right, was the Transporter bridge, spot-lit and shining a pale, unworldly green. I stared warily at the river, leaden and sweating a dingy vapour. Everything so real, so concrete, ugly and—

The change was faster than instant, no hint of transition. Nor was there any semblance or parallel to the Newport just gone. The thought amused me. What had I been expecting? Some kind of shadow Newport—past, future or somewhere in-between?

I closed my eyes, held them tightly shut. What had I been expecting? And the answer was a cold Newport night and a full English breakfast at dawn. A moment later. I opened them again and looked out upon a bleak and unfamiliar landscape.

It was night here, too, the bay narrow and enclosed on both sides by black jagged cliffs. Behind me, half hidden by a few dishevelled dunes were the shadows and hints of unnatural architecture, a settlement of some sort, but one I knew instinctively to be avoided. A silver strip of beach separated me from the sea. It rolled heavily like molten iron before crashing, then fading into sand.

I remembered what Jack had told me. *You must be standing in the exact same spot if you ever plan on returning.* I squatted, careful not to move my feet by the breadth of a hair and traced their outline deep in the sand. I dug my finger in even deeper, a delicate furbelow of sand marking its progress as once again I traced around first one shoe, and then the other. Satisfied at last, I lifted one foot and then another, turned and stepped aside.

At the same time. I became aware of a quiet whispering, almost lost in the soft roar of the sea. It seemed to be coming from the sinister outcrop behind the dunes. Feeling like a victim in a horror flick but impelled by the same curious desire to confront what was there, I walked in a hesitant, weaving pattern towards the nearest dune.

Gradually the buildings of this strange city became more sharply defined, creating an impression of a sinister, monochrome maze. There was a degree of uniformity in the tallness of both walls and buildings, the narrowness of the streets, but there was, too, a sense of decay, as if it might all fall down at any moment under the weight of its shadow. As I approached, the whispering grew louder, the streets a little more narrow, and I sensed them willing me to walk further and deeper into the maze. The whispering stopped and was replaced by an oppressive silence that was far more frightening. I felt their eyes upon me, and imagined them, rat-like, gelatinous, and ravenous; these souls, dead in themselves, would strip me to the bone and yet remain as empty as ever.

The thought was worse than any nightmare, and I turned and ran back to where the sand looked cleanest. Immediately the whispering resumed as though my presence had already been forgotten.

I returned to the rock, and repositioned my feet in the patterns I had made for them. I searched the inside of my jacket, locating an old pocket watch nestling in a bed of used tickets and ancient receipts. I was confident that its sturdy, Edwardian mechanism would still be functioning, but I wondered how closely its time would relate to this realm, and whether dawn would actually break It was 1:20 a.m.

The water was still so it looked almost solid. And I scanned the horizon, focusing on that fine strip of darkness that separated sky from sea. They will come, Jack had assured me. They come every night, hunting for nourishment, a ghastly treadmill as they scavenge for souls or what's left of them. I imagined aborigines rummaging the sand for pale desert grubs, and then something more immediate had come to mind.

"What about me?" I'd asked, "The tethered goat on the shore."

Jack had smiled. "You are alive, in the land of the dead. To them you're barely a ghost. Don't worry."

Now I wondered. As I stared into that leaden sea, different, more sinister pictures entered my mind. I saw the souls of long dead Vikings—sea-wolves and pirates treading through darkness, a hunger that could never be sated.

I closed my eyes and opened them again. The horizon remained as blank and featureless as before. They will come, Jack had said, and I believed him. It was at that moment I was aware something watching me.

Instinctively I turned, scanning with dread the sand dunes behind me. The dead souls had sensed my presence. I had been foolish to explore. Don't leave the rock, Jack had said. Now, emboldened by number, they were somewhere in that darkness hunting me, knowing I had nowhere else to go.

I stood there for a moment or two, studying the dunes for any flicker of movement, and I heard behind me the sea breathing, like some vast animal biding its time. I swivelled round and dropped into a crouch. Nothing. And then I saw the cause of my fear.

To my right, between where I was standing and the sea, was a large, misshapen rock. And I knew with quiet certainty that it, or something hiding in its shadow, regarded me with malevolent intent. I approached it cautiously, repeating Jack's words like some kind of mantra: *You are alive, in the land of the dead. To them you are barely a ghost. Don't worry.*

The rock was grotesque, embodying in its form the suggestion of numerous entities welded into a reluctant whole. It looked as though it might once have been gelatinous but had calcified in age and salt. Clustered around it were smaller jelly-like creatures. At first I thought it a trick of the moonlight, but as I watched they wavered and shifted in form as though each component struggle for a memory of what they'd once been. I saw faces, some baby-like, others old. From one, a large beaked head emerged, and then a wing, before a score or more pale and desperate faces pulled it back in selfish act of collective will.

Slowly I retraced my steps, occasionally looking behind me for fear they were following.

Not until I was safely back on my rock—which I now examined carefully, did I wonder where they'd come from—what they were. I studied the beach about me, noting now what I hadn't seen before. There was a pattern to their size and distribution, and it was clear that they'd emerged from the sea. The smallest were closest to the waterline, and they increased in size as they neared calcification.

I checked the time again. 2:50 a.m. and once more fixed my gaze upon that dark space separating sea from sky. This time I was rewarded as the first shape emerged from the darkness. Within moments, the horizon crawled with them. They loped across the surface of that dead, ash coloured sea as though it were a basalt plain, and as they approached the air thickened, so that they became dim shadows in a hot reeking fog.

Now they were upon me, long limbed and sinewy, dingy and furred. And the smell became even more intense; a stench so foul and terrible it seemed to cling on me with a life and hunger of its own. Sweat poured down my face and neck. I felt my throat tighten until it became difficult to breath. Without thinking, I rose from the rock and ran through them, desperate to immerse myself in the coolness of the sea from which they'd come. I caught glimpses of rounded heads reminiscent of seals and eyes that glowed with an unholy light. One snarled at me, unseeing but sensing that something was there.

And then I was at the water's edge, teetering inches from a thinning crest of yellowish surf. Cautiously, I stepped back, realising almost too late the menace in that sinister swell. Thousands upon thousands of those strange gelatinous creatures bobbed in the ebb and flow, suspended like small oily slicks, feeding on what the ocean gave.

Now I was sweating for a different reason, as I realised what might have been. The sea would have drained me, providing sustenance for what it carried, turning me in time to one of them.

Something made me check my watch. I wrenched it out from its pocket and saw with a start that time really did work differently here. It was 4.49 a.m. Where the hell had those two hours gone? Dawn or its equivalent might come at any moment.

The beach now was empty, but from the darkness behind the dunes the whispering had been replaced by a horrible, wet slavering. I raced back towards the rock. I was sick to the stomach with fear. What if I had left it too late? Within what I thought were moments I was back at the rock. My watch told a different story. Another fifteen minutes gone, but the worse horror lay directly beneath me.

The passing of so many greylings had trampled and scuffed the pattern I'd made in the sand. Where was I to stand? I stared down at the ravaged beach in something approaching despair and thrust the watch back into my coat. The horizon was black, but for how long?

From the corner of my eye I saw the jelly-like creatures moving towards me. They looked like slugs and, although slow, their progress was relentless, their purpose clear, and me with no means of escape.

Quickly, I knelt down, fighting back panic. I scanned an area little more than the size of a small coffee table. It may as well have been the Gobi desert. And then I saw two things: a glint of gold and, just to the right of it, a tiny curl of braided sand.

I picked up what could only have been Jack's signet ring. Then, gingerly, I placed my foot in the sand, matching the thin curl to the curve of my shoe. Common sense told me where, approximately, my other shoe should be, but approximate wasn't good enough. There was silence now in the dunes, and I knew that the carnage had stopped.

Work it out... work it out... I glanced again at the horizon, imagined that it was a little more grey, then turned my attention to the ground one final time. I thought back to how I had gone around the pattern a second time, digging deeper, and remembered how my finger, responding to the natural weight and balance of a squatting body, had exerted most pressure as it curved around the heel. I narrowed my search still further and was rewarded by a faint indentation—mine or that of a Greyling.

Frantically and knowing I had no time to hesitate, I positioned my heel in the indentation and stood. At the same time, something touched my shoulder—a Greyling, its hot, rancid breath a burning drizzle.

I turned my head, watching as it circled me. A tongue suddenly snaked out of its mouth, wet and black and slightly sticky. It coursed down my face. It smelt of seaweed, despair, and felt like slimy sandpaper. Then it flickered across my body as though assessing shape and size.

I stood motionless, like a rabbit in the glare of a stoat. Its eyes were now narrow slits, and I wondered whether it was trying to focus on what it couldn't see. The Greyling brought its face close to mine; nostrils, small and perfectly round, quivered and sniffed, and then slowly it drew back its head, and in its eyes I saw indecision, greed, and something that frightened me more.

I watched, unable to move. Saw its muscles tense, hair stiffen, and closed my eyes as its jaws opened to reveal teeth like densely packed needles. Those teeth were a stark but brief image, for what stayed in my mind were its eyes. They had the blank stare of the scavenger, one that has sensed something just out of reach; but there had been more... an implacable conviction that this would not always be the case, that tomorrow, the next day, or some day after that, I would be back, and it would be waiting.

My legs and thighs were wet and warm, the trickle extending down to my socks. What did it matter? I opened my eyes slowly. I was standing on a quayside. The merchant ship had gone. The river was a dingy brown, the sky sombre, almost black. A motorbike growled softly in the distance. It was then I saw Jack.

He was curled up in the shadows. At first I thought he was asleep, and then knew, almost before touching him, that he was not. His face was cold and he was smiling, as if somehow he knew. Gently I pushed the ring onto a finger that was already stiff.

An iron gate clanged and there were voices in the warehouse behind me. "Goodbye Jack," I whispered. I thought of the cheque, and wondered what time it was. I delved into my pocket, feeling the sharp outline of Jack's cheque, but other than that, nothing. Angrily, I dismissed the urge to panic, searching each and every pocket systematically and twice over. I was sweating. Panic returned, and with it despair. I allowed it to wash over me. The watch wasn't there. I stared down at Jack, the glint of gold on his left index finger, his peaceful smile. It was hard not to kick him. I raised both hands to my cheeks, knowing already that they would feel somehow alien, and that I would find the experience unpleasant.

Bony Park

"Are you sure this is the best spot, Rick?" Robert had serious doubts. He looked up at the sun and then at the steely surface of the lake.

"Why what's wrong with it?" The younger boy sounded defensive.

"Oh, nothing. It's just that—well its pretty hot now and likely it'll get hotter, and there's not much shade here."

Rick nodded and looked around. Robert was right of course. Worse than that, they were close to the path, and there was a bench nearby. "It'll be busy later on what with the zimmies."

"And joggers."

"Winos... Thing is, do we take the tent or leave it here?"

Robert sighed. "I don't know; let me think." In the cool twilight of the previous evening they had picked what seemed to be a good spot, their tent sheltered by bushes in a small but natural bay. Now it was evident they'd made a strategic mistake. They were just too close to the path. Serious fishing would be out of the question. Robert looked behind him. It was still early in the morning, and the path was already occupied.

A middle-aged man was turning the corner. He carried a paper in his hand. He was smiling. The crunch of gravel grew louder, its rhythm remorseless.

"Morning, boys!" It was a cheery voice, the voice of a man pleased with himself, pleased with the day. He waggled his paper—"Beautiful morning," and walked on by.

"Morning." Robert smiled automatically and stared at the silent water. This was the wrong spot.

Rick grunted. "Wanker." The sound was barely audible. The man stopped and turned around.

"You're in the wrong spot, you know." Pleasantly, as if it didn't really matter, but there it was. He paused and wiped his brow with the hand holding the paper.

"Over there," he said, pointing to a small wooded headland to their right. "Small cove, just like this, but shaded, that's where you'll find the fish. Used to go there myself—when I was a young'un." He looked round dubiously and pursed his lips as if in thought. "Picnics and barbeques by lunch time on a day like this—screaming children all over the place. Fish? You'll be reeling up toddlers!"

The boys laughed. "I've never gutted a toddler." Rick said.

"What about the tent?" Robert glanced sideways at the taut blue fabric, quivering in the early morning breeze.

"Leave it."

"Can't do that. It's not ours. Anything could happen." The three of them studied the tent in silence. The man coughed sympathetically.

"You're right. Can't just leave it, especially if it doesn't belong to you. Look, I'll tell you what, it's on my way. I live just past the gate." He pointed to a distant glint of metal, the chimneys of some newly built houses half-hidden by trees. "How about I show you the place, and if it's as good as I say it is, well then move camp. It'll be worth it, I'm telling you, boys." Wasting your time in a spot like this ... unless you want tiddlers and chips."

"Toddlers," Robert shouted.

"Toddlers to you, too!" The man chuckled.

"You go. I'll guard the tent." Rick started reeling in his line. "Call me if it's any good."

Robert nodded and stepped onto the path alongside the stranger. "Is that the paper, there?"

The man looked at his paper and then at Robert. His eyes twinkled behind glasses. "Yes," he said.

"What I mean is does it have last night's score?"

"United? Yes, I suppose so. Here, take it." The two of them ambled along the path towards where the fishing was better. Robert, immersed in the back pages, stumbled several times. He was jabbering in excitement, or indignation. The man didn't appear to be listening. Rick looked at them until they turned the corner and made a decision. Any place had to be better than this. He'd get the tent packed in readiness.

"There you go." The man's voice was calm.

Robert squinted at the bushes.

"The path's just beyond. Look you can see the lake from here."

Robert stared over the gleaming foliage. Just beyond was water, a shimmering tongue poking into a dense cluster of willow and ash. The man pointed with his paper towards the gate. "Right, I'll be off, then."

Robert hesitated.

A crunch of gravel. A smile. Followed by a tap on the head with the newspaper. "Come on, then, follow me." The man sounded resigned.

The two of them pushed through the bushes, displacing sunlight and green metallic-looking leaves.

They stopped on a thin strand of gravel and sand. A gloved hand wrapped itself around Robert's throat; fingers, lean leathery hounds, worrying, shaking, digging their way deeper into his flesh. The lake, pale and sparkling, blurred into a bluish smear. The boy's legs lost contact with the ground; a mountainous weight descended on him, and his face smacked into gravel.

The man regarded him in quiet anticipation. Where to make the first cut? He knelt, scrutinising the boy's neck. There—just below the ear, a small mole. Still uncertain, his knife hand moved down, pushing a small dark curl out of the way. He had to be certain. It had to feel right. Be right. Thumb and forefinger touched the mole tenderly, stretching the skin in readiness for the first cut. *Ohh yes! Do it... do it—do it—do it.* The voice was urgent, impatient.

Robert opened his eyes. His lips widened into what would have been a scream.

The sign! A change of target. Steel, finely honed and shining, rammed into the boy's open mouth, slicing savagely this way and that, pressing right the way down, until the point scraped against bone. It felt right. He grabbed the boy's hand.

Rick was sweating, his shirt wet and sticky, clinging on to his back. Every part of him prickled, and his head felt heavy with heat. A headache was coming, either that or a storm, or both. Every so often, he shaded his eyes and stared down the path. In his mind, he saw a cool, tree-shadowed cove, and he wondered why Robert was taking so long. But the job was done. Tent neatly packaged with rods firmly attached. In the distance, he heard a faint shout. A man was waving a newspaper at him.

He picked up the tent, adjusted his grip on the rods and trotted eagerly along the path.

Tom Baxter

> *This is a 'true' story as told to me by the brother of the bus driver when I working in a biscuit factory. I have merely embroidered some details...*

John didn't have much to say that day and was glad the driver, Sam Dawson, seemed in a similar state of mind. It helped that it was the first bus out, and so far there had been no passengers. Things would be different an hour or two later when rush hour began. John tightened his lips. In his view, passengers had too much to say on just about everything: a missed penalty, a bent referee, occasionally politics or a scandal in government.

It wasn't good enough that the person behind, in front or alongside were dragged into the debate. The bus conductor had to express an opinion too; and John didn't want to express an opinion, on anything. Last night he'd run down a girl on a bicycle and driven away. A 'hit and run' merchant. They could ask his opinion on that.

The girl had shot into Malpas Road near the Harlequin roundabout, and he'd hit her full on. Sound and image blurred: a coat, pale in the headlights, arms flapping, the crunch of metal and crushed bone. John shook his head, focussed on the greyness beyond the slow-moving bus.

"You all right, mate?"

The question startled him, and John grunted, attempted a smile and continued his stare through the window. There was magic in these roads, the streets that led off them, an otherworldliness that came with decay. In bright sunshine they looked out of place. Only at night or in winter, melting in greyness and rain did they seem both mysterious and right.

At 5.30 am, and swamped in a raw rainy wind, their mystery became even more intense, their rightness more sombre. The wind gusted and blew, and a sudden fierce volley of sleet swept the road, sending cartons scuttling like dim crabs into gutters, where they drowned in long puddles of silver and black.

Why had he drunk so much? He asked the question often. One day it would be the death of him—it should have been the death of him—not a small girl who'd jumped the queue.

He wondered about the family, whether she had one. Of course she had: a father and mother, a brother waiting at home. He pictured them, the knock on the door, two policemen, the cup of tea without which a death didn't signify; it would be heavy in sugar. It always was in films. Why wasn't this a film? Something to walk away from like nothing had happened.

"Irish tea, toast... eggs, bacon, tomatoes, fried bread..." Sam was rhapsodising unconcerned as to whether John shared his fantasy.

Despite himself John intervened. "You've already got toast there."

"I know."

"*And* fried bread."

"I like fried bread."

John slipped back into trance as the bus inched its way to the docks. The wind was picking up, occasionally shaking the bus as it navigated roundabouts or corners.

Newport seemed empty, its buildings dream-like as they drifted by. Through steamed up windows the town consisted of shadow, the occasional tree, skeletal and gaunt; streetlights orange like barley drops, edges blurred in rain.

Another thirty minutes, John thought, and Sam would have his fantasy breakfast, while he would sip strong tea and think of the girl he'd killed just hours before.

The rain was pouring down now, splashing off huddled cars, overflowing gutters, and turning grey, twisty streets into things glimpsed in dream.

At first John didn't see him, stopping Sam barely in time as a shadow materialised into a figure tentatively waving. The bus crawled to a halt and the doors opened in a sibilant whoosh.

An elderly man dressed in a long tweed coat and peaked cap stood there, as though waiting for something other than a bus. Ex-military, John guessed, taking in the neatly clipped moustache, the ramrod-straight bearing. John reached out, guessing the old man would have trouble navigating the high step from the kerb.

The hand was leathery, the air wet and fresh. The old man shook himself and water scattered and dripped in fine pearls of light. John shivered and stepped back, allowing the man to pass and walk upstairs to the top of the bus.

Sam waited, allowing the old man time to ease himself into a seat, before driving off. Sam was good like that. John recognised it. Other drivers—careless, malicious or sometimes bored—would drive off on the instant, causing the unwary to tumble and sit where they landed. He wondered what Sam would say if he knew... then shoved the thought to one side. It was done, the moment gone and that was that. The girl wouldn't come back, and he wouldn't dwell.

"I think I'll join you in that breakfast, Sam."

"You feeling better or what?"

"Guess so. Drank a skin-full that's all."

"You need a wife, lad. Keep you on the straight and narrow."

"When I want straight and narrow, I'll marry a bloody tram."

"Okay, okay. Just saying."

"A quiet run."

"As quiet as it gets, son. You'd better see about that fare."

John pulled himself up the stairs, hands gripping chrome, his pouch and ticket- machine bouncing slightly as he ascended. His first reaction was uncertainty followed by shock. The man wasn't there. His gaze swivelled from front to back. The deck was empty, the floor clean. He wouldn't be hiding under the seat. Old men didn't do that. Nevertheless, John found himself walking the length of the top-deck checking each and every seat.

At last he gave up, walked down, scanned the downstairs cursorily and admitted defeat. "Sam... there's nobody up there. Nobody on the bloody bus except us."

"Don't be bloody daft. Of course there's somebody up there. I heard the old feller go up those stairs, waited until—"

"The old feller sat down—I know—but I'm just saying; there's nobody up there now."

"He's probably died on us curled up on the floor or something." Sam brought the bus to a halt and cut the engine.

"Only he hasn't. There's no one up there."

"And you're a bloody dick-head, John. What are you?"

"Dick-head, and you're a fucking soft-arse. Come and see."

John stepped back and made way for Sam in much the same way as earlier he'd made space for the old man. He gave Sam a few seconds start and then followed him up the stairs. So he hadn't gone mad. Sam remembered him, too: a tall, gaunt man in a long tweed coat and matching peaked cap. A scarf, too, he remembered, a neatly clipped, grey moustache. He couldn't remember the eyes.

"Bugger me," said Sam, "and there's something else, too."

"What you on about?" said John, checking the windows, pretending he wasn't. He felt stupid; bus windows. These were particularly small, glorified letterboxes even a budgie wouldn't squeeze through.

"The man was dripping," said Sam. "We both saw him. Soaked right through he was. I'm telling you, there was no way he'd walk up here, sit on some seat and not show it. Do you see any drips, a puddle, any wet or damp at all? If he'd sat down he'd have left a bloody great piss-stain."

"Yeah, okay, okay. I get it. A man came on the bus, didn't get off and now he's not here." His voice echoed in the glass and metal shell. He should have been excited. A ghost. I mean that's what it came down to. A bloody ghost on the docks bus. It wasn't right—not on a green Atlantean with its chrome and new leather smell.

He should have felt excited. But he wasn't. He felt uneasy, sick, the butterflies heavy and desperate in his stomach and chest.

Sam's face looked yellow in neon light. "I can't believe it. It's happened to us. It's happened to *us*." He sounded excited. A pain stabbed through John's head and with it a sensation of something crawling through it.

John sat, sipping his second sweet tea. The table, blue Formica but chipped and stained, was surrounded by half the depot, some standing, others on chairs arranged in a close but irregular circle. Sam had finished the story, John emphasising that no way could the man have got off without passing them—that there'd been no other passengers—and that the bus hadn't made a stop until *after* they'd discovered the man wasn't there.

The third man at the table, an old driver who should have retired some years before, tapped his pipe and nodded agreement prior to saying anything. "Tom Baxter, sure enough," he said.

"You just don't expect it," said Sam. "I mean, I've heard of him, but you don't expect you're going to see him... that it's going to happen to you."

"*What's* going to happen to me?" John replaced his mug on the table, careful to keep his hand steady.

The expert on all things ghostly sucked on his pipe for a moment or two and said nothing. He patted his groin, leaned his weight on the table and stood before weaving his way to the toilet.

"What's going to happen?"

"Nothing likely, Sam said. "Don't worry about it." He put his hand on John's shoulder. "Old stories passed down."

"Old don't mean false," another man said. He eased his way into John's vision, an elderly conductor running to fat. His lower lip glistened.

"Tom Baxter was real alright—one of us—drove buses."

"You're saying we saw his ghost?" John remembered the neatly dressed man, the touch of his hand.

"War years it was. Blackout, you know the score." The conductor paused. "Hit and run. Very nasty business."

"Tom was run over?"

"No, not Tom—his daughter. Couldn't have been more than five. Tom was walking her home. The car came from nowhere."

"And it wasn't a hit and run," another voice said. "The guy stopped, Yank by all accounts, got out of his car. Handed himself in when the police came, and then Tom, Tom did a very strange thing. He stood up from the corpse of his child and shook the man's hand."

"He forgave him? Find that hard to believe."

"And so do I—and maybe he didn't. Some say it was more of a curse. The following day that same Yank was found by the roadside, only he wasn't a Yank anymore, not even human—not in a real sense. You ever see anyone rabid? This was worse by all accounts. Man had become an eye-bulging, slobbering lunatic. They found him shrieking and babbling, snapping at flies, at anything that moved."

"And that happened the very next day?" John said, the pain in his head a slow, steady burn.

"Aye lad, it did." It was the old man, returned from the toilet. He lowered himself into the chair left vacant for him, his eyes hinting he knew more than he should.

"Stories," Sam said. His voice sounded less sure.

"Likely as not," the old man said. "And anyway, it's not as if you shook hands."

A Touch Of Rat

There are worse things than herpes.

January 1981

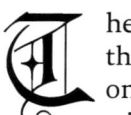

The scratching was getting on his nerves. He lowered the book and looked down the derelict room. It had once been a bar, panelled in walnut and studded with red, velveteen seats. It had once been the home of the serious drinker, less serious hookers, and students who read about both. It was also where he'd lost Suzy, and where he feared he would see her again.

Lloyd cast a final, lingering glance down the long room of shadows. Behind him, Newport's traffic rumbled fainter as evening deepened. A street lamp threw a square of orange light through the small window above, and he wondered whether he'd stay this time.

It was the scratching that did it, every time the scratching. He'd try to ignore it, douse it in logic. The ruined building was tucked into a side street next to the market and surrounded by takeaways. There *would* be rats, lots of them, bound to be. And it was always that thought that drove him away.

Tonight would be different—like previous nights had meant to be. Then, as now, Lloyd had come equipped with flashlight and gun, a flask of coffee, another of brandy. "I'm ready," he murmured—as loud as he dared.

He leant against the damp panelling, breathing in mildew, and tried to recapture a moment in time: the long copper bar, drink-puddled and stained, the Mynah bird that never talked but peeped through a brown tobacco haze, large women in tight dresses, laughter and smoke, lots of smoke; and ensconced in the snug, the four of them waiting to score.

June 1980

The door opened as if Suzy had been waiting for him on the other side. They stared, each assessing the other, half-smiles widening. Suzy looked as Lloyd remembered—slight, olive skinned, plump in all the right places, dark-eyed and intense. She wore an ivory coloured blouse and a pair of expensive looking jeans. Lloyd felt his dick stir even before Suzy rushed into his arms and pressed close. Her hand glided down his spine and slipped into his back pocket. Her fingers were warm and moved slowly up and down.

"Lloyd, you haven't changed. You look—you look wonderful." She stood back, allowing Lloyd to squeeze past a bit at a time. Her eyes shone in excitement and something else, something more chemical. Lloyd didn't mind. Suzy still wanted him and he felt good about that and, for some reason, a little uneasy.

She released his back pocket with a pinch and pointed to the living room, a pale green space fresh with daffodils and a few Victorian prints. At the entrance they stopped. "Would you like some wine?" Suzy nodded in the direction of a small table where a vase had been pushed to one side, and replaced by a bottle of red and two glasses.

Lloyd shook his head. "I'm fine thanks."

"Whatever." She shrugged and stepped back, studied him more critically. "It suits you, your hair short like that."

Lloyd smiled. "It's because you've become old and respectable."

"I have, haven't I." She brought her head close, her mouth brushing his cheeks.

Afterwards Lloyd stared, numb and content, barely registering the dusky-pink room, the over-sized bed, rumpled now and stained. Why was he here? Why had he come? Lust... and what did that say about his marriage?

Curiosity or boredom? Boredom he decided. Suzy was exciting but not a tart he could blame, though she was that and more. No, he was the villain here, discontent with his sweet, easy-to-please wife.

Alison.

Even the name was sweet.

He'd liked that at first, until he realised what lay behind. Emptiness hidden under a thin, sugary crust; Alison was empty, had nothing to give.

"Lloyd?"

"I'm sorry—miles away."

"I asked why you came?"

"Revisiting the past?" It was a feeble line and Suzy saw it as such.

"That's funny," she said. "And what does that make me?" The smile disappeared. "Nostalgia on the side?"

"No." He'd offended her. Shit.

Suzy edged closer. "It doesn't matter, Lloyd. I'm glad to

see you... and as for Alison." She reached out, her hand stroking his cheek. "You've made up your mind."

Lloyd said nothing. He sensed what Suzy would say next—if not the exact words, their direction and sentiment.

Suzy grinned. She touched Lloyd's shoulder. "Alison is pretty enough..."

"I know, and we're happy *enough,* but..." Lloyd stopped. "But not close."

"Shall we talk about it later?"

Suzy gave a lazy smile, moved closer and rested her chin on Lloyd's shoulder. "I'll go run you a shower."

Lloyd nodded. Alison would know. She was empty but not without instinct. Even if there were no possible way of knowing, somehow deep inside she'd know. Would he mind that? Wasn't this what it was all about?

"What are you thinking?" Suzy had stopped at the bathroom door, was looking at him.

"Oh, I don't know." He lied. "Happy I guess."

The shower was hot. He made it hotter and stayed in as long as he could. One of Suzy's towels was draped conveniently near and he wrapped it round his shoulders, enjoying its warmth, its Suzy smell.

Suzy looked up from the bed and raised an eyebrow. "You look good. Come here. Come on! I'll dry your hair."

Lloyd shook his head, moving to the couch where he'd folded his clothes in a neat pile.

"You sure you want to go?" She sounded amused.

"I have to."

"But you don't want to. Good." Suzy walked over, pressed her hand against Lloyd's cheek. "I'll see you out."

At the door she hesitated. "I'm meeting some friends this weekend. You could come along, if you like."

As simple as that.

Two sentences that would change his life and hers.

January 1981

Her friends. Just names, now: Roz and Mike. Both dead ... but not Suzie. The thought made him tremble. Then there was Lascar. He'd be around, possibly close, creeping up on him behind the long bar. Lloyd grimaced, prayed he was wrong. Either way he'd find out soon enough.

Lascar had seduced them with promises, holding the small balls of paste in his hand. He'd watched as each in turn had swallowed them with beer. Only Lloyd had refused, and Lascar had sneered.

"You'll lose her." He nodded at Suzy. "You won't keep up with her."

It had been hard, or rather it hadn't been hard enough.

September 1980

"I don't mind. You know that." The tone, a patient whine, suggested otherwise, and always she pleasured herself after he'd done—again and again. And more and more, she begged him to change his mind, to take the pills should Lascar return.

"It gives you bad dreams," he said. "I've seen you. Sometimes you squeal."

She grinned. "Does that turn you on?"

"You turn me on," he said. And it was true. True for everyone she passed in the street. "Better than that Viagra," Lascar had said. "You want it, and those you touch want it too."

Touch didn't come into it.

"Pheromones," Mike told him. "There's a joke there somewhere."

"You're thinking of 'Whore moans' and I don't think you can."

"Can what?"

"Make a joke from it."

It wasn't a joking matter. All of them now, all except Lloyd, exuded irresistible appeal, Suzy especially, and yet she stayed faithful. Lloyd wondered for how long.

"We should go to that pub again."

"You mean it?" There was hunger in her voice, relief, too.

"Yes. I want what you're having." He didn't, not really, but the alternative—losing Suzy—was worse.

Lascar was already there, sitting as though he'd never left. Suzy handed over the money and each in turn gulped the small glistening pellets. All except Lloyd.

Suzy's hand strayed to his knee. She edged close to him, waited.

This was it then.

"Still scared?" Lascar's tone was aggressive.

"No, but I'd like to know who I'm buying from. We know nothing—about you—about this." Just saying it hit home how ridiculous it was, the risks they were taking.

Lascar, a tanned, lean faced man in a baggy track-suit and sporting a grey pony-tail, thrust out his hand with compelling authority, and Lloyd grasped it, noticing too late, a peculiar gleam in the other man's eye.

"*Henry* Lascar."

Lloyd barely heard him, caught in a grip that made him feel vaguely unclean. Lascar's hand was greasy, like oiled rope, and his fingers bristled though not a hair was to be seen. There was something terribly wrong with this man, and if sense prevailed he should have drunk up, made his excuses and left.

Instead he chewed the glittering pellet and drowned it with Guinness.

January 1981

Lloyd flashed the torch, its beam slicing the darkness, creating new shadows. He opened the brandy, brought the flask to his lips. Through half-closed eyes the bar came alive again, and with it a smell, musty and feral.

The smell brought past and present together, as had the dream that jolted him awake just three weeks before.

The smell was Lascar's. Lloyd had noticed it from the start. Suzy later had the same smell. Now he had it, too. He put the torch on his lap and pressed down, struggling to retain his nerve, wanting more brandy but unwilling to drink it too quickly. The scratching was all around him now, in ceiling and wainscoting, even the floor. Lloyd leant back, trying hard not to scream. He wouldn't run. Not this time. Not anymore. He closed his eyes, focusing on memory, every last scrap.

September 1980

"What is it—exactly?" Lloyd felt stupid. He should have asked earlier—before swallowing. "Where does it come from?"

Lascar coughed, leaned forward, reached for his drink.

"It's not important now."

"It's important to us... isn't it?" Lloyd looked round for support.

"I mean," said Lascar, "that it doesn't really matter—not now."

"I think you *chose* us," Suzy said, more intrigued than alarmed. The light caught her L'Oreal black hair as she moved closer, and Lloyd imagined Lascar's hand stroking it. His stomach clenched in revulsion.

"Why?" asked Mike.

"Why?" There was a sneer in Lascar's voice, and

something else; hopelessness perhaps, something he was trying to hide. "Is that the same as 'how'?"

"Okay *how* did you know?" Mike's eyes were febrile bright, his gaze sweeping the bar with lascivious intent. "How did you know we were looking to score?" He stared at Roz, as though about to jump on her. "I mean we were looking to score, but not this."

"Cannabis." Roz said. "Coke."

Lascar grinned showing large, yellow teeth. "It's a seamen's pub. Everyone's looking to score."

"You're a sailor then?" Suzy edged closer, flirtatious, already on heat.

"I travel—Far East mostly—Borneo ... China. India." He spat out the word: India.

Lloyd leant forward, eager despite himself. Television had packaged much of the world, but beneath the dense high-rises and squalid, teeming streets he knew an older, darker 'East' prevailed.

Lascar read his mind and shot him down in flames. "The East is shit," he said. "All of it."

He spoke with such venom that Lloyd sensed a woman, perhaps a man, was somewhere involved.

"Something happened in India. What?"

"Deshnoke. You heard of Karni Mata?" He looked at their faces. "No. But you've tasted its secret. A girl showed me it."

Something in his tone made Lloyd put his drink down. "Girl?"

"I like them young," Lascar said. "She was a beggar, worked the temple."

"And the secret?"

The laugh was short, resembled a squeal. Lascar leant forward. "Oh, the secret." He extracted several more glistening pellets from his pocket and let them roll across the table. "'The fruits of Karni Mata.'"

"Yes, but what are they?" Suzy asked, her curiosity aroused.

"The main ingredient is not very nice, but it's more than that, much more." His voice rose to a falsetto: "'A gift from Durga,' she said, as she fed them to me like grapes."

"The other ingredients—the magical ones—she wouldn't tell you," Lloyd guessed.

Lascar nodded. "Killed her trying to find out—not purposely, mind." He glared at Suzy and Roz, and again the yellow teeth showed. "Only she knew. She knew what she was doing. Bitch!"

"We do drugs," said Suzy, drawing back. "We don't comfort killers. Not child-killers"

It was a brave thing to say but Lascar showed no offence. "I'm not here for comfort." Again that peculiar gleam in the eye. "Too late for that."

"Why, did she come back to haunt you?" Roz sounded angry and hopeful.

"She didn't have too." He paused. "But something did... at night... there were noises... scratching."

"Scratching?" Roz sneered. "Rats, you're afraid of rats?"

"No, dreams," said Lascar, "and what happened afterwards." His tone was flat as if the dream and what followed had lost their terror. His eyes though were sharp, even hungry, looking at each of them in turn... assessing.

"Dreams?" Suzy sounded worried.

"Only they weren't dreams," said the stranger. "Not in the end."

"Tell us about it," said Mike. "We're listening."

Lloyd winced. Mike never said much, and when he did it was crap. Now he sounded like *Frasier*. Worse he had just placed his hand on Lascar's knee in some kind of weird, male bonding.

The table rocked, as though someone or something was shaking it, and the smell grew intense—musty and feral, sharp.

Lascar grabbed hold of his beer, apologising with a glance. "It comes and goes," he said. In his face Lloyd saw resignation and fear.

Mike intervened. "No harm done. Epilepsy is it?"

Again Lloyd winced. The man didn't answer, sipping his beer instead. Lloyd hastened back to the topic. "Tell us about it—the dream."

"It began as a dream; then became real."

"What did?"

"The rat... I was holding a rat."

Suzy looked sick, Mike open-eyed and intrigued. Roz's face was impassive. "You held a rat?" she said.

"And it wasn't a dream. I could see every greasy hair on its body, its pink feet scrabbling air, its tail thrashing. But that wasn't the worst of it. I could feel it, squirming in my hand, stretching and bunching. The thing was warm and alive, throbbing, its mouth stretched in a horrible snarl. And then it pissed down my arm and I wanted to let it go, but couldn't so I ran to the port window still holding the damn thing, its piss steaming, running down my hand and arm."

Bloody wet dream, thought Lloyd. It must have shown in his face.

"And I know what you're thinking," the man said. "But you'd be wrong. It wasn't that."

Lloyd let it pass.

"Rats are lucky," Mike said.

"I'm glad you think so." The man stared straight ahead, through the door that led into the main bar. His lips quivered; his eyes remained dry as though every tear had been shed, and Lloyd again felt afraid, but didn't know why.

"You're saying something bad happened." Roz's voice wavered as though it was a question she hadn't meant to ask.

"Soon after that the growth appeared."

"Cancer—that's tough, mate." Mike leant forward. "You

think the dream was a warning, your body or subconscious telling you something?"

The table vibrated, the stranger barely able to control his movement, and the smell intensified. He's losing control, Lloyd thought. He's bloody shitting. Lloyd tried to stand. The man's frantic stare held him in place.

"You want to know what's coming to you?" the man was panting, his face suddenly taut in pain. He pushed back his chair, hands grappling with a tracksuit rippling like a small earthquake. The table tipped over, glasses toppling this way and that, and none of it mattered. The man's mouth distended, and the panting grew harder, more urgent—the sound punctuated by a wild, frantic squealing from somewhere below his stomach.

Lascar ripped down his track-trousers, and a rat the size of a small dog shot out, gaining purchase on the edge of the table—straining but going no farther. The table juddered and the rat continued to squeal, its head jerking in hunger.

Roz and Suzy were holding each other, white-faced, too terrified to scream. They edged out the door, pushed on by Mike, all of them staring at the rat tugging out from Lascar's groin, its tail lost in a mass of dark, wiry hair. It glared back, sniffing, catching their smell.

Lloyd pressed against the wall, his escape partly blocked by the lunging rat. Its host stood flaccid, mouth and eyes opened wide as one witless. He looked deflated, all energy and life consumed by the monster now rocking the table in its effort to break free.

January 1981

Horror had come to them that night, smashing the glamour Lascar had promised. Roz though put it into words: *'We're not bloody monsters, right. We can do something about this.'*

Shortly after she vanished, taking Mike with her. Lloyd and Suzy grew closer but said little. They lived in her bed, rutting in her dusky-pink room. Occasionally they scavenged discarded takeaways.

And then Suzy vanished.

Lloyd fled the Welsh rain, blurring the dreams in drink-induced stupor—but never the appetite. He needed Suzie. He needed to fuck.

It was in Italy he heard the news. He checked The South Wales Argus website for details: 'Suicide in Newport pub.' Two bodies had been found—well not even bodies. Both had been reduced to charcoal close to where he now sat. He could see it, or imagined he could, a dark, irregular patch on the dust-coated floor.

His first thought had been Suzy, and he remembered sighing with relief; jewellery and teeth had identified the couple as Mike and Roz. He wondered about them, envied their courage. It would have been Roz, definitely Roz. *'We're not bloody monsters, right. We can do something about this.'*

The pub had never re-opened, but the rat population had grown larger. He heard them now, scampering with intelligence... waiting.

Shadows deepened as did the smell. It seeped through the walls and flooring, the brown ceiling bulging with age. He was aware, vaguely, that the scratching had stopped, knew they were waiting. This was it, he realised; there could be no running away, not now. He'd known that in the early hours of the morning, his already deformed penis heavy and swinging—autonomous.

A squeal shattered the silence.

His balls jerked violently from side to side, and pain sliced through flesh and nerves as something obscene strove for its freedom. It had begun this morning: butterflies in his stomach, spiders in his balls. The spidery tickle had changed into something more vicious, and he imagined small feet, stubby and pink, scrabbling in darkness, his testes swelling in the shape of two bristling haunches. He was afraid to look down.

Instead, Lloyd placed the gun on the table. *'We're not bloody monsters, right. We can do something about this.'* He wondered whom he'd shoot first, the rats as they came for him, or the thing he was feeding. He wondered about Suzy. The thought made him tremble.

Such A Night

Inspired by a Vegas wedding

"Are you sure?"

"I am if you are." She leant her head against his shoulder causing the Retro to swerve.

"Not now!" He tightened his grip on the wheel. "Tonight, goddammit. We've paid good money for this."

"Elvis..." She sighed. "It's going to be so romantic."

"I liked the younger one."

"Black leather?"

"'68 yes."

"I'm sorry, Tom, but you asked me, remember, and I want him in white leather and sequins... He had more gravitas then."

"He had more weight."

"I wonder when he's finished like, I wonder if he'll wipe us with his neckerchief. He used to wipe his brow with them and throw them into the crowd."

"It would be a nice sacramental touch. I'd like that."

The bridge arched into the distance, Wales a smudge of white in the haze. Registration had involved forms, fifteen of them, all referring to something called the Welsh Autonomous Region. Tom smiled. Jo had cackled when she'd pointed out the acronym. *'That's not very romantic. Maybe we should have asked Hitler instead.'*

"What's up? You're grinning like this is funny or something."

Tom's grin grew wider. He swallowed a calm-aid. "I was just thinking how much I love you."

She sniffed. "Just as well... considering." She placed her hand on his knee and squeezed.

God, she excited him, had done so from the moment she'd walked into his life.

Walked into his life—a rhinestone cliché—a bit like their destination and their final renewal of vows. Clichés were good, he thought. Effortless.

"They should know by now." He kept his voice even. For some reason the thought made him nervous. He'd always hated being talked about.

"What—you mean back home? Of course they'll bloody know. Your lot will be spitting hairs."

"They're Christian. Nothing wrong with that."

"They're reverts. Always on about duty."

"No problem with duty on *your* side."

She looked at him sharply, said nothing. Tom focussed on the road. She was sensitive about family, but it was true. The entire Macallan clan were free spirits, freebooters, free everything. They talked of *rights*, inventing them at the drop of a hat.

His lot, the Darts, were no better, God fearing and dour but as greedy, focused on duty, family, inheritance: Montagues and Capulets growling over bones.

Last night he'd wavered but Jo had proved firm. 'We're going,' she'd said. 'Don't think about it. Don't worry.'

Jo was right. They had to get out.

They were entering Chepstow, what was left of if after the clearance. The castle still stood, probably good for another thousand years. It seemed almost part of the rock. The rest of the town consisted now of two or three streets, each house whitewashed, some showing off geraniums. Artificial. It was the same through much of the south. Unsustainable for all but the rich, water more precious than gold.

"It looks pretty," she said.

"It is. Once we're past the reserve, it'll get even prettier."

She pulled a face. "Reserve—sounds nice, but I've seen the pictures."

"Yeah, well, it should have been, but clearance on that scale..." He left it unsaid. Most of Newport and Cardiff were underwater, outlying areas reverting to swamp. Not so much ugly as melancholy, a grey and red Venice sinking lower and lower. He passed over the cream. "Repellent, you'll need it."

"Can't have Elvis kissing mozzy bites." She nodded at the slurry below, "What else do you reckon is down there?"

"Apart from some strange looking jellyfish—nothing. The occasional methane flare—and bloody mosquitoes!" The car swerved again, as he slapped his arm a fraction too late.

"How long do you reckon?"

"Till we get there?" He glanced at his watch "About four. We'll have the evening to settle in, have a look round. When did we book the ceremony for?" He tightened his hold on the wheel, anticipating the response.

She gripped his knee and squeezed till he winced. "You peasant. You unromantic peasant!"

Tom watched her sleep, her face grey in shadow. He knew he could watch her forever, knew that wouldn't happen. It was time to wake her. He postponed it a minute or two longer.

"We're here," he said.

Jo opened her eyes. They were blank for a time, and then she focused and scanned their surroundings. "Oh, Tom... it's absolutely gorgeous."

"Welcome to Merthyr Park."

They overlooked a wide gorge studded in olive trees, their leaves metallic in a low, slanting sun.

"Chapel of Love's just down there," Tom said.

"So this is it then. No going back."

"No going back."

The Chapel consisted of four rose-coloured domes, a fusion of concrete and glass. Cypresses framed it in long green shadows, Tom pointed at one of several pools, turquoise chips that gleamed and looked ice-cold. "How about a swim before we look around?"

"And then the zoo," she said. "I'd like to see the zoo before we go."

They had the Savannah to themselves, along with wildebeest, zebra and lions. Forests marked the eastern horizon; to the west a shimmering dome marked India and the lands that surrounded it. A shadow swooped from the sky, and Jo flinched, grabbing on to Tom's arm.

"A vulture," he said. "Unbelievable, it looks so real."

"Yeah, well, we know all about vultures." She grabbed his arm. Look at that. I mean, how do they do it?

At first he didn't see it.

"There," she hissed.

The grass rippled in a sudden breeze, and Tom froze as two alien eyes fixed upon him. The lion snarled, its lips peeling back. It bounded towards them, muscular, tawny, leapt through the air. Yellowing fangs and blood coloured tongue, the smell of stale meat. Tom hit the ground.

"Fuck it—gerroff!"

Jo laughed. "Coward. For fuck's sake *you're* supposed to protect *me*." She rose to her feet, pulling Tom up to his. "Where's he gone?"

"Vanished in pixels," said Tom, both exhilarated and ashamed. "God, that was good. I mean that was real. Really real."

"Maybe you'd like the lion—instead of Elvis."

"And miss out on the sacramental neckerchief, or towel thingy."

"Not necessarily. You get what you pay for."

"A lion in a white jump-suit—"

"—glittering in Rhinestones, why not? One for the family album."

"Keep them talking, that's for sure," Tom said.

"That and the bill." Jo giggled. "God, they're so going to hate us."

Tom kissed her full on the lips. "Only we'll be somewhere else."

"On a slow boat to... where?"

"Does it matter?"

"Suppose not. I like surprises." She popped a calm-aid in her mouth, tossed the empty pack on the ground. A monkey materialised from nowhere, retrieved it and vanished.

"Do you think real animals were ever so cooperative?" said Tom.

"Well, they're pretty much extinct. Some would call that cooperative." Her voice was sharp, extinction clearly touching a nerve.

"It'll be time soon."

"I know."

"Do you still want to go through with it?"

"Tom, that's so bloody romantic. Do *you* still want to go through with it?"

He kissed her. "I can't imagine life without you. Bring on Elvis and to hell with the lion."

She slipped her hand in his. "I'm sorry. I feel bad. Elvis, it was my idea we could have had... Monroe."

"Too fat."

"That's cruel—okay then, Cleopatra."

"What did *she* look like?"

"Well who then? Who *would* you have liked?"

"You," he said.

"You're a weird boy. I mean think of it, *me* giving us away... giving me away."

She looked troubled. Tom placed an arm around her shoulder, pulled her close. "Joking. Elvis is good. Anyway, *I* asked you, remember."

"And I said... yes."

Tom noted the hesitation, brought his face close to hers. "So you get to choose."

"Elvis... flowers."

"An eternity of bliss," he whispered.

"Who knows... perhaps, but I do love you, Tom. Always will."

Jo felt quivery, passive... greedy. She smelt roses, lilies and something earthy, more dangerous. She breathed in again, hard and fierce, and her head swam in darkness, and the ground disappeared. "What's happening?"

"Treated air. *Eternal Night,* I believe."

"Very sexy."

He stood behind, one hand covering her eyes. His other hand rested on her stomach, pressing her into him until she felt his excitement. "Can I look now?"

His hand shifted from face to neck, and she opened her eyes.

"Bloody hell, so this is it then."

"Pleased?" He sounded anxious.

"Of course I am. It's beautiful... It must have cost."

"We're not paying, remember."

"No, we're not paying."

She scanned the room; no, not a room, perhaps a space, its shape and size suggested by a dense cerise carpet that seeped into where walls should have been but weren't. She glanced upwards. No ceiling, just the suggestion of something endlessly deep, endlessly red.

A heart-shaped shadow dominated the room, an ebony void one could sink into. Its edges wavered in a warm, perfumed breeze.

"The bed," he whispered. "Come on."

"Where's Elvis, I mean what happens now?" She felt nervous, excited yes, but nervous. His fingers were tugging at buttons on her blouse. *For God's sake!* She pushed him away. "I want Elvis."

His lips tightened.

She was spoiling things. "I'm sorry. I want you. I just wanted Elvis to... participate."

"Elvis will do whatever we ask him to do," said Tom. "Even the tacky."

A quarrel, she sensed it hovering over them, now of all times. "Look, Tom, I'm nervous, in fact I'm fucking scared, ok?"

Tom sighed. "You're right. I'm sorry." He looked at the bed, began undressing himself. "He comes when we're ready, I think."

Jo watched him for a second or two, then slipped out her clothes, lying down beside him on the bed. She took his hand and pressed into him. She'd read about old time drive-in burger-bars, drive-in weddings, had thought them tacky. Not this though. This was class.

"Where is he?" she whispered.

He squeezed her hand in reply. "There. Jo, over there! My God, he's fantastic!"

"It must have been like this when those old guys had visions," she breathed. "I mean, it's like Jesus, or God or something... an angel... do you think he can hear us?"

Tom said nothing. Jo continued to stare. He was real. She'd studied CGI, had grown up with holos, but this was solid; this was real... She imagined his fingers, his lips brushing hers. God, if he touched her she'd die! The thought aroused her and made her giggle.

His hair was perfect, glossy, black, with a suggestion of blue; and the white leather jump suit glittered in diamond and pearl. For a heavy man, he walked with grace, and he was looking at her, not Tom, at her. She breathed in deep and fast, breathed again until she was panting. *Treated air... Eternal Night? That was it.* Tom panted beside her, his excitement matching her own. And now Presley stood over them, pagan and bronzed, his breath dense and sweet.

"Jo and Tom we are here to day in the presence of God to

sanctify a life of grace with the gift of eternal love. Tom, do you take Jo to love in death as in life?"

"I do."

"Jo..." Her mouth opened. She stared at his lips, sardonic and full, searched out their fallen-angel curl as his words fell upon her. "Do you take Tom to love in death as in life?"

"I do?"

"Then with the authority invested in me by the Welsh Autonomous Region, I now pronounce you legally dead." He bent down and kissed Tom on the brow. His lips moved towards Tom's neck, putting her in mind of a vampire.

Come on!

He bent over her and kissed her hard on the mouth. Jo writhed, hot under his weight, Tom's grip weakening then falling away. The prick was faint, almost not there, and a warm numbness spread through her.

She was dying. Thirty years of marriage come to this. She wondered when she'd stop breathing and whether she'd notice, and the planet—would Elvis sing for that, too? Her lip curled, tried to. Her body felt dry and stiff like salted fish.

Their children wouldn't have a happy inheritance, whichever way you looked at it. Well sod them. Sod them all—their expectations, their hints, their greed, their impatience. Resentment, she thought, Tom's side especially—all strait-aced and dour. They wanted them dead not hanging around essentially useless. Never said so except in the occasional sidelong glance, talk of inheritance dressed up in laughter and smiles. Well sod them. There was no inheritance. Not now. The Chapel didn't come cheap; neither did Elvis. She heard his voice, haunting and mellow, recognised the tune, smiled at the words.

Raggedy Man

There was such a man but his story is different.

Peter watched him pass, checked the time and followed him. It wasn't a difficult task. Newport's centre consisted of a road leading directly to the docks. What had grown around it had been peripheral, side streets leading to nowhere. Now, with industrial decline, that straight as an arrow road led to much the same place. Peter increased his pace, confident his quarry lacked any sense of his presence, and uncomfortably aware that the raggedy man was faster and fitter than he'd ever be.

No time for window shopping or ducking in doorways, Tramper—what the kids called him—was running now, something he always did as he approached where Commercial Street split. Here he either ran left into Church Street or slewed to the right down Alexandra Road. But before that he paused, almost as though hoping there might be an alternative.

On one occasion, Peter stood opposite him on the other side of the road. He observed his quarry's face drawn in confusion and pain. Moments later Tramper raced left into Church Street like someone approaching the finishing line before juddering to a halt as though crashing into a pane of reinforced glass: a ring road, Usk Way separated them from the docks; the only view traffic and beyond that scrubland, railings and galvanised sheds.

He'd stared wildly, long coat flapping, as though seeking somewhere different. He ran backwards and forwards like a moth demented by flame, then he'd turned, ignoring Peter, retracing his steps to where the road forked.

Alexandra Road offered more choice with streets peeling off from it: Mill Parade, Coomassie Street, Brunel Street. But all choices ended in the finality of the ring road, a steel and concrete noose that obviously baffled him.

Today he chose Alexandra Road, careering down its several streets, stopping each time at some mysterious barrier, and then turning back.

There was magic in these roads, Peter thought, an otherworldliness that came with decrepitude. In bright sunshine they looked out of place, even the new-build. Only at night or in winter, melting in greyness and rain did they seem both mysterious and right. But Tramper looked for something more and every day never found it.

Peter stopped on the corner of Brunel Street and watched Tramper approach the Transporter Bridge, which dominated streets and ring road alike.

Victorian built, it looked more and more alien every time Peter observed it. Metallic and graceful, it swept over the river and made the buildings beneath look shabby and small. All except one: the Waterloo Hotel.

Tramper was staring at the hotel, as he did every day, muttering and shaking his head. Peter stayed put. The pattern never changed. Tramper would retrace his steps, lose energy like a clock winding down before vanishing into a side-street hostel to recover his strength.

Not yet though. Tramper was cursing, shaking his fist at the ring road he clearly thought shouldn't be there. Every so often he ran at it, sliding along an imaginary barrier, like a mime artist playing with glass. And then he disappeared. Peter blinked. Impossible.

He ran the hundred feet or so to where Tramper had vanished, working out the only possible explanation. Tramper had changed his pattern. He'd turned the corner whilst Peter had blinked.

Peter walked the final few yards and looked to where he assumed Tramper had gone. Tramper stared back at him, and Peter started, then smiled, as though to a stranger. He placed his hands in his pockets and turned, inspecting the red-tiled turret of the Waterloo Hotel. It was a fine building, yellow bricks turning dark red as it ascended.

Was Tramper behind him still, waiting to challenge why he'd been following him? Peter didn't turn, instead continuing his inspection of the Victorian Hotel and one-time brothel. What fascination did it hold for the raggedy man?

Peter focused his gaze on the brick trellised turret. It possessed a grace and magic similar to that of the bridge, the red-bricked latticework with its diamond panes of black. He imagined it in moonlight, gossamer threads spinning from it, solidifying into strands—reaching out over the road; creating new worlds.

A cough behind made him jump.

"Do I interest you that much?"

Peter swivelled and stepped back. Tramper followed, his face now inches away. Peter swallowed hard, unable to say a thing. He'd been prepared for this moment, in theory at least, but now, assailed by a smell of oranges and tobacco and a bulbous-nosed, unshaven face, the words didn't come.

"Are you one of those 'do-gooders' or is it something else

you fancy?" Tramper leered, pushing a strand of grey hair away from his cheek.

Peter forgot the words, remembered the truth. "People talk about you."

"I know they do—they call me raggedy man, smelly-arse, old Tramper. I've heard them."

"So why do you do it?" Peter jerked his head at the ring road, the lorries thundering past.

"You don't know?" He looked disappointed. "I thought perhaps..."

"Perhaps?"

"I thought you had the answer," Tramper said, his tone combining defiance and defeat.

"No," said Peter. "Curiosity. Simple as. I just want to know."

"You mean you're a nosey arse."

Peter shrugged. "Least I'm concerned." He wasn't. Both of them knew it. "And I also know you're afraid of the ring-road."

"You think that's it?" Tramper's voice thickened in anger. "Afraid of a road? Listen, boy, that road shouldn't be there. It has no right being there. There should be—" He jumped back and stood on the kerb, his back to traffic "—something else there."

"For God's sake!"

The raggedy man teetered, and Peter strained to grab him.

Tramper grinned. His eyes remained dead. "Do you have children, Mr Nosey-arse? Because you won't have much longer." He launched himself backwards into the road. Peter hesitated, knew it was already too late. A furniture van screeched unable to curb its momentum. Peter closed his eyes. A voice, hoarse and threatening clawed through his mind.

"Watch out for her. Won't do no good, mind."

"Lucy? How do—?" The words stopped as a van squealed,

and he saw two faces, one grinning. A squalid crunch erased the grin in a tangle of fabric, and then it was over. Peter lifted his gaze to a face in the van freeze-framed in horror.

So that was it then? Peter stared at what remained of Tramper. Tragic. Prosaic. Mystery solved. Tramper had lost a child here. Just that. Flowers attached to a lamppost probably—and after that unable to let go. In a way he couldn't explain, Peter felt cheated and winced at his own tawdry response. Shock. Almost certainly shock. The driver was talking at him, jabbing his mobile. Other cars pulled up. Not many. Peter nodded: a local tramp. Suicide. The driver couldn't have done a thing.

Peter paused at the door, squeezing Tramper from his mind. He rang the bell, and then again. He heard the thump of feet behind the heavy mahogany door. His neighbour lived by 'Good Housekeeping'. She had energy and taste. More importantly, her husband had money. Inside, the house was awash with fabric and pine. A Laura Ashley home.

The door flung open and Lucy hurled herself into his arms. "Daddy, lovely Daddy." Rachel hovered in the doorway. Smiling.

"She's been as good as gold."

"Thank you, Rachel. I'm very grateful." And he was. He liked Rachel, and so too, did Lucy, an impeccable judge of women and dogs.

"Would you like a coffee or anything? The kettle's on..."

Lucy nodded vigorously "Oh yes. Go on, Daddy, say yes..." Her lips were pursed in a pleading pout that said more than words. He groaned. She was only five. What would she be like when she was say seventeen?

Rachel smiled. "See you tomorrow then, Lucy." Lucy

buried her head in Peter's shoulder, waving a sulky leg in lieu of goodbye.

"Thanks again, Rachel."

"Oh that's all right. When's Allie due back?"

He sensed a hint of suspicion in the voice and smiled, amused at Rachel's craving for news, preferably bad.

"In a few days—with a bit of luck. Bye."

"Bye. Bye, Lucy." The door shut behind them. Lucy gave a mighty sigh.

"Do the camel walk!" She ordered, and Peter obeyed in relief. They bounced in synchronicity, brushing past overgrown privet that tried to join in. "What's for tea?"

A whisper. Another good sign. The key to Lucy's heart was her stomach. Peter grinned at the thought of a key-shaped stomach.

"Fish and chips."

"Oh goody." She snuggled in closer. "Lovely Daddy."

Peter let her slip gently as he fumbled for the key. He stroked her summery hair, his fingers rough with affection and she looked up, large grey eyes staring at him appraisingly. She put him in mind of Elizabeth I only Elizabeth's hair had been auburn. Lucy's hair was a fine pale gold, searing in sun.

"Come on, Bess!"

"Who's Bess?"

"Elizabeth Tudor... Elizabeth I of England."

"Was she nice?"

"When she smiled, it was pure sunshine that everyone did choose to bask in if they could..."

"That's nice. That's me"

"But anon came a storm from a sudden gathering of clouds and the thunder fell in wondrous manner on all alike."

"What does that mean?"

"She could be a bad tempered little hussy."

"Huh! Did you make that up?"

"No, a man called Sir John Harington... He went on to design a toilet, I think"

"Hmph! What would he know about anything... But was Elizabeth nice, really?"

"She could never make up her mind. In you go, puppy."

Peter kept TV on that night as a means of forgetting. He switched it off when the Welsh news came on, switched it back on again when it was over. Even so, Tramper inveigled his thoughts. At last the evening—Lucy's part of it—came to an end. Peter decided on a book and some whisky after she'd settled. He needed it. Tramper would resurface, but diluted with alcohol and filtered through strong narrative, the thoughts might be manageable.

"Right. In your pyjamas. And if you're quick, a sweet before bed."

She regarded him thoughtfully. "I do not like being bribed."

Peter winced at his glibness, hid a smile at the moral response.

"Quite correct, Lucy. You're right. I was wrong." He put her down and opened the door.

"That's quite alright, Daddy. Just get me a sweet anyway."

He smiled. She was his daughter again. "Milk, Super Ted and ... a sweet."

"Two. Two sweets."

"Two sweets," he sighed.

"Three—"

He shut the door pretending not to hear. With a bit of luck... supper... five minutes ... teeth and story fifteen... and the rest of the evening his, a book and some whisky.

"Right, up to bed."

This time, as if sensing the urgency he was trying to hide, she replaced argument with a single demand.

"Carry me."

And he did, wondering suddenly what his life would be like without her.

"I'll put on the light. I'll put on the light." She grabbed at the string pull, and hurled herself onto the toilet.

Peter glanced at his watch.

"I'll be quick." She sighed, wiping her bottom with vigour. Then, standing to attention and giving him a salute, she opened her mouth and then shut it with a sudden snap. He moved closer cupping a hand gently below her chin, raising her head, until he could see her eyes gleaming with mischief.

"Right, Lucy, open your mouth." She refused. It was one of the many rituals that bound their lives together and gave Peter the raw happiness that made every day worthwhile. "OK then!" He grunted and tickled her nose with the toothbrush.

"That's not my teeth, Silly!"

Peter popped the brush in her mouth before her mouth had time to shut. Sometimes she sucked the toothpaste off, but not tonight. Tonight she cooperated. The initial cleaning done, she took the brush and made her way to the sink for the final rinse. Peter approached her, brush in hand. She regarded him warily, waited until he had started, and then:

"That is not *how* you brush a girl's hair, I can assure you!"

"Assure me? You can assure me?" He looked at her, amused beyond measure. "Lucy, Lucy, where did you come from?"

She thrust her fists into her waist. "I came from America! In a parcel this big!" Her arms stretched out as far as they could. She regarded the space in-between dubiously. "Well as big as I am anyway."

She caught a glimpse of her reflection and paused, hands falling. She stared hard at herself in the tall mirror.

"Will I be even more beautiful when I grow up, Daddy?" Peter laughed at the blatant vanity.

"Yes, sweet-heart. I expect you will." She smiled, satisfied, and regarded herself once more.

"Yes, but do I look more beautiful here…?" She looked at him earnestly. "Or do I look more beautiful in the mirror?"

Peter lifted her up, enjoying her weight, the warmness beneath the soft pyjamas; she smelled of fresh bread and toothpaste. He looked into her bold blue eyes and kissed her gently on the forehead. "You can't do this to a mirror."

She looked at him, mildly exasperated. "Of course you can. Look." She wriggled from his arms and planted a firm and noisy kiss on the glass.

"That's your lips. *I* kissed your *head*."

He allowed his daughter five more minutes to plant a kiss on her reflected head before switching off the light. "Time for bed."

Lucy followed him, picking up a small pink mirror on the way.

"Right, what story do you want then?"

"I want Mummy to read my story. Oops!" She giggled, "I forgot. Mummy's with Grandpa tonight. When is she back?"

"In a few days, love. Until then you're stuck with me."

"That's alright, Daddy. I like the way you clean my teeth. Now what story shall we have? Ummm." She pursed her lips, pretending to look thoughtful, then held up the book she'd been reading all week.

"You want this one," said Peter, taking "Lucy's Dragon" from her grasp. Lucy grinned and snuggled down into her bed so that only a glimmer of hair and eyes were showing. Then, suddenly the duvet was thrust to one side. "I'm hot!" she said. "Can I sleep on top of the bed—under your dressing gown? Can I, Daddy? PLEEESE!"

Peter smiled. The robe was made from warm red

towelling and was a stock item in her dressing up games. More importantly there was a half bottle of whiskey and a book waiting to be reconciled with an early night.

"That's a good idea—but no story." The afterthought made him feel small and mean, but in his mind was a warm fire, a book and a room to himself! The 'no story' would give him those extra few minutes.

Lucy smiled, triumphant, and bounced on the bed into his arms.

He left her clutching the dressing gown, her eyes following him as he left the room.

"That's right—leave your lovely daughter for a book."

He paused on the stairs.

"What are you reading then?"

He smiled. "It's about a man who has a black jewel stuck in his forehead."

"To make him look pretty?"

"Bad men have put it in there so they can control him. It's a kind of camera."

"Why can't he just cover it up with a hat or something?"

"Do that and the jewel will come to life and eat into his brain like some mad and voracious insect."

"That's gross."

"Pity we can't get one for you, sweetheart."

"Oh shut up." A pause. "Thanks for the story."

"Any time."

At last. He left the lounge door a little bit open, and switched the coal-effect fire to medium. Bottle. Glass... Book?

Peter made his way to a dark mahogany bookcase, its shelves filled with paperbacks, their spines pristine. Book found, he eased himself into the Parker Knoll, pushed it nearer the fire.

It was 12 o'clock when Peter awoke. "So much for an early night," he mumbled. His throat felt tight and in his mouth a harsh and sour taste. His arm stretched for the whisky, knocking his book on to the floor in the process. "Time for bed, most definitely time for bed."

Peter groaned and pushed himself up from the chair. The room was peaceful in shadow, the way he liked it. He liked especially the fire and felt sad turning it down and then off. He crept into the hallway, its gloom alleviated by a sliver of moonlight from a window halfway up the stairs.

In the bathroom he saw Lucy's toothbrush on the floor. It puzzled him. He replaced it in her container, sat on the toilet and relieved himself of the day. It was in that position, chin resting gloomily on the cupped hands, knees reddened from the weight of supporting elbows, that he heard a low muttering from Lucy's bedroom. For a moment it chilled him he realised she was talking in her sleep. He wiped his bottom thoroughly; it was for him a minor obsession that demanded copious amounts of paper. He imagined each sheet as an end of term reportnand continued his wiping with a new, ferocious vigour. His fingers closed on the chain—*Don't wake up Lucy*—and pulled.

Peter closed the seat and waited for the noise to diminish, then opened the bathroom door. He tiptoed into Lucy's room, focussed his gaze on a bed blurred in shadow. A moment—one he would afterwards strive to remember: A face, warm pink and sleepy, a flash of pale hair. And then gone, the dressing gown, blood red in the gloom, filling her space.

The mind can play tricks. Peter bit on the fear, the chill that made it difficult to stand. He clung on to the door and shut his eyes. When he opened them again, she would be there. She had to be. Then his life would return. "Please, God. Oh, Please, God. Make this a dream." He felt the sweat dripping down his arms and spine, and opened his eyes. The blood red dressing gown sprawled sullenly on the still empty bed.

He knew it was stupid—bloody—bloody—stupid.

"Lucy..." a whisper.

He poked the dressing gown, lifted it up, searched every pocket, explored every crevice and finally buried his nose in the warm material breathing in deeply. There was the faintest fragrance, which he sucked in until his lungs could hold no more. And then he sat on the bed and cried.

He was going mad. Lucy had vanished, blinked out of existence before his very eyes. There was no point in searching the house. No point at all. But he did. His cries echoed in shadow and gloom, and he thought for a moment he could hear others, other voices shouting back in protest.

Peter knew what had to be done but not how to do it. Allie would be fast asleep, unaware of the nightmare about to shatter her dream. He found the phone, fingers stabbing clumsily on to numbers barely seen. It was like stabbing at shadows, nothing real any more. The absence of a dialling tone added to the futility. Peter tried again, and finally in desperation, the operator.

She at least was real. A disembodied voice momentarily shared his darkness. "What number do you require? Which town...?"

He clung to her questions hungrily, delaying his responses, aware the nightmare would return in force as soon as her questioning stopped.

"I will connect you now..."

Peter waited, drawing in breath.

"I am sorry, sir. The number you have given me does not exist."

The voice, only moments before normal and comforting, sounded now shallow and horribly shrill.

"Of course it does you bloody, stupid, woman." *Of course it did.* He waved the barely seen phone at the shadows surrounding him. Her parent's phone number had provided their lottery numbers these past two years. Their phone number had won them minor prizes on three consecutive occasions. Their phone number was lucky, indelibly engraved in his head. She had made a mistake. He placed the receiver back to his lips. Perhaps they'd changed numbers, gone ex directory. But the bloody, stupid woman and her shrill had voice had gone.

Police then. The thought made him fearful, and he hesitated, then reached for the phone. Its shape seemed different, more clunky, but the voice that answered sounded thin like the one before.

"Police."

"I want to report a missing child."

The phone dropped soundlessly on the hall table and Peter made his way to the fridge. He pulled out a four-pack, and returned to the living room.

He had barely finished his second can when he heard a car stop outside, then brisk clipped steps on concrete stairs. The doorbell rang. It sounded faint, unfamiliar, as if some how it came from a different house. Peter stumbled from the chair and pulled himself through a grimy corridor leading to the front door.

"Peter Noak...?"

"Yes, yes—come in." He was crying.

"I'm W.P.C Bradshaw." A policewoman put her arm about him and led him back into the bed-sit.

"I'll make some tea," she said. Her arm loosened, and Peter glimpsed a young, capable woman leave the room, switching on a light as she did so. A yellow glare scoured the dusty room, throwing into relief the greasy pink curtains hanging on unwashed wood.

Peter stared at his hands, fingers digging fiercely into the faded sides of a beige and pink chair. The chair was familiar. Everything was. But it was not *his* room. Not his room.

Air burned his lungs, and he found himself gasping like a fish pulled from water. His heart thumped in his throat before hitting his stomach. He clutched at his chest.

"Where am I?"

A uniformed officer sat on the sofa facing him. He looked uncomfortable, inexperienced, as if he wished he was making the tea and the woman doing the questioning.

"Deakin," he said. "Constable Deakin. You reported a missing girl—your daughter?"

"But she wouldn't be here, Officer. We don't live here!" Peter's voice rose to a shriek. The policeman leant forward. He had a young, foxy face, accentuated by cropped red hair and a small moustache. *He's here to catch chickens!* And Peter laughed, a horrible thin tittering sound he tried to stifle between tight-latticed fingers.

Deakin grunted and squeezed next to Bradshaw on a sofa that sighed dust.

"Feeling better are we, Sir?" Not too bright; soft and neutral, the tone just right. Peter looked up from the rim of his cup into the eyes of WPC Bradshaw. She had dark eyes as deep as wells, a fresh face.

She reminded Peter of a country squire's daughter. He stared at her, imagining her squeezed into hunting pink, her rounded bottom bouncing rhythmically on a large chestnut mare. He saw her in a Jane Austen drawing room, dark eyes sparkling mischievously behind a lacquered fan. Saw her in thin fabric, high-waisted and bare armed; creamy breasts cupped in a low cut bodice.

His tea was cold. And he was in the wrong room.

"You reported a missing child." She prompted.

"Yes," Peter put his cup down on the thin carpet. "But..." He looked round helplessly. "This isn't my house. I don't live here!"

"Perhaps you would show us the child's bedroom."

"Yes. Yes!" That was the heart of the problem. If he could find it. "Follow me."

"And where is Mrs Noak?" Peter half turned in the poorly lit corridor. This was not his house.

"Allie? Yorkshire," he said. "Her father's got a dicky heart. She's gone up for a few days. He does well... but we all get lonely at times." His voice was his own at least, but the words seemed unreal, as strange as the house.

They walked to the end of the corridor in silence. Ahead of them was the kitchen, its door half shut. "Mind these two stairs now. Always catches people out..." Peter stopped. How did he know that? This wasn't his house. In his house the living room opened on to highly polished stairs that wound their way up past a large stained glass window. In his house there were flowers, and a daughter that growled and bullied and pulled at his cheeks.

Deakin's voice intruded. "How did you know—what you said about the steps? This isn't your house, you said." Courtesy hiding a sneer.

Peter stumbled into the kitchen wearily, and recognised where he was. A pale blue Formica table; he scanned the room in a glance; grease splattered stove, unwashed frying pan, windows grey in dust. The nightmare solidified.

"I used to live here..." his voice was a whisper. "Fifteen, twenty years ago."

Deakin and Bradshaw joined him at the table.

"Look!" His fist closed around the small Spider-Man figure in his pocket. "Look. It's Multi-jointed Spiderman!" He placed the small shiny red and blue collectible on the Formica surface where it poised, in gleaming arrogance, peering inquisitively at nothing. "It's Lucy's. It proves I'm not mad. I'm telling the truth." He could tell by their faces it didn't, that for Deakin in particular it confirmed beyond doubt that here was a sad dangerous lunatic.

"You're telling us that you are married with children. And your wife is in Yorkshire."

Peter nodded wordlessly.

"And you woke up to find your daughter gone and

yourself transported into a bed-sit you vacated fifteen years ago."

"I'm not mad," said Peter.

"No one is suggesting you are, Mr. Noak." The woman, she had a nice voice. Peter looked up gratefully.

"Have you phoned your wife yet...?" The voice soft and probing.

"Yes." His throat tightened. "But I couldn't get through. I tried the operator and she couldn't find the number, said it didn't exist."

"And where did you phone from, Mr Noak?" Deakin's damp foxy face moved closer.

"Why, from... here." Peter's voice wavered. "Look, I know this sounds stupid but I phoned from here, only here isn't here any more!" He was angry. Shouting. "Anyway you can check with the bloody operator. She'll have a record won't she?" The three of them stood, Deakin's watery blue eyes staring hard into his.

"There isn't a phone here is there, Mr. Noak. You've been wasting police time."

"You're wrong. You must be. How did I phone you then? How did I phone you if there's no phone?" Peter heard himself babbling; knew none of it made sense. There was no phone here, not in this squalid room. Never had been. So how had he called them?

"We'll look into that." Susan Bradshaw smiled, eyes alive with sympathy. "Good-night, Mr. Noak. We'll see ourselves out."

Peter followed them to the door, every so often glancing upwards where stairs should have led to a large stained glass window, a turn on the landing, and then his daughter's bedroom. Now he saw a lightbulb, bare but for a thin drift of cobweb hanging from its cable. He closed his eyes and the door at the same time. The bulb, a burning dazzle imprinted on his retina. In darkness and from behind the closed door he heard the two policemen talk.

"I've seen his kind before." Deakin sounded matter of fact. "You smell the whisky on him?" Then: "I think he fancied you. Couldn't keep his eyes off. Staring he was."

W.P.C Bradshaw chuckled. "I noticed. Bit of a sad-case."

Despite himself, Peter fell into a dreamless sleep. He awoke determined to put things right but without knowing how. He shaved, using a razor he'd found in the shared bathroom, avoided the toothbrushes. The towel looked dirty, but he dried himself down after a perfunctory wash, dressed and went out.

His home, an Edwardian redbrick, was in a parallel road. He'd go there first. Lucy would open the door, and he'd make some kind of excuse about having gone out to see friends. She'd be outraged, censorious, bound to tell Allie everything; how daddy was drunk, had gone out and left her alone. And Peter would grin, suck it all up, delirious, relieved.

The road at least was where he'd left it, but as he approached the house his stomach turned. The giant conifer wasn't there. Gone too was the privet. An elderly lady opened the door as he knocked, and the look she gave made him wince. What could he say? 'I used to live here—I do live here—this is *my* house.' She'd phone the police and they'd recognise him and lock him up for wasting police time. Peter cried. Watched her close the door.

He spun round—Rachel—she'd recognise him. A white UPVC door dashed his hopes. A pair of damaged Venetian blinds in an adjacent window confirmed what he already knew. There was no Rachel, or if there was, she didn't live there.

Peter lay on his back staring at an archipelago of damp on the ceiling. The mattress was hard, the whisky almost gone. Earlier that day he'd had an idea—the school where he'd worked for over a decade before an engineered redundancy. But institutions had continuity. There'd be people there who'd know him, children he'd taught who'd now be in Year 12 or 13.

The school was five miles away and involved several hills, but that at least would be there... For God's sake, a school doesn't move.

Only this one had.

He'd stared for several hours at a small, neat housing estate squeezed into what had once been a school and a badly designed play-ground. His life had been erased and with it a family, *his* family.

Raggedy man grinned. *'Watch out for her. Won't do no good, mind.'*

That night he dreamed. He sat on a bus. Lucy was close, as yet invisible. Outside roads and buildings slipped by, more vivid, more magical. The bus drove slowly along Newport's main street, drifting left into Church Street, which seemed longer than he remembered. Now he was walking, Lucy besides him, holding his hand. There were workshops yellow in light, green-painted doors, small alleyways and shops that belonged to another, richer, happier time.

Lucy smiled at him and then faded, and he was on the bus again, sleep-crawling on Newport's road to the docks. This time the bus veered right, as he knew it would. An old, yellow and red-bricked hotel loomed and slipped by—and the road continued with nothing to block it. He looked down on ruby-bricked houses with sharp silver roofs. The streets glowed moonlight blue and writhed in slow, sinuous harmony. Somewhere he heard Lucy crying. And he awoke, alone on a damp greasy bed.

At once he leapt to his feet, blazing in hope. He pushed back the curtains, and scanned aging terraces brown in rain. He thrust on his black, raggedy coat and rushed out the door. The answer was here to be found—in Newport, its streets.

The Devil's Mirror

They say that staring too long in a looking glass is the surest way to invite the Devil into your heart. So here I am, mirror propped next to the screen, and me staring into it like a model from Vogue.

Only I don't need a mirror to sense what's inside. Whisky sometimes does it, but the effect is inconclusive and short lived. I want to *see* the Devil, not hear his voice in my head. I want my friends to see him.

My friends.

Hey, Zak! Seeing you clearly, buddy. The voice is faint. I turn up the volume and *'buddy'* echoes across the shadowy room. Buddy. We're strangers, voices in the dark, net-friends.

"I wondered when someone would come. I've been staring at this thing for an hour."

Sorry, old buddy, webcam's wonky. Seeing you good now—right profile at least. How about me? Sorry. You're going to keep on staring into that mirror right?

"Until the end."

Neat... A new voice.

"Who the shit, are you?" Word was getting round. Seems like mention the Devil and you suddenly have friends all over the world. That's the theory. So far all I have are two strangers, randoms from nowhere.

Captain Bob, reporting for duty. So what's the deal?

Hi, Bob, name's Simon—Sly for short.

"Welcome to you both—and to anyone else lurking out there. The deal is simple. Just watch me."

Sounds cute.

Sly or Bob, I couldn't tell. "I'll be sitting here, staring at my reflection."

Your alter ego.

Bob, I think. Pretentious sod. "And I'll be tapping my thoughts, what I see, what I feel onto the keyboard. You are my guarantors, my witnesses. It may be a long evening, but I promise you there will be an end, one way or another. But no more talking from me. It breaks the mirror-spell. And you don't speak unless you have to. Just be with me. I will *write* my every thought—a kind of online testament. You two…"

Will be there for you, Zak. Isn't that right, Sly?

That's right. Just pretend we aren't here. It's just you and that crazy old mirror.

Just pretend you aren't there. Right. Just stare at the mirror; tap down what comes.

Don't see you writing, Zak… ah. Okay, you've started.

Shush. Sly, sounding concerned.

If I'm honest with myself, fear pure and simple stopped me from doing this before: testing a possibility, a way out of everything. 'Stare too long in a looking glass and invite the Devil in,' something my mother told my sister when she was young. Both dead now, but the memory stuck. The temptation came later but tempered by fear. Even now, a voice whispers, *you're going to be sorry. You're going to be sorry…* on and on, like a child keeping time to its skipping.

Wonder what Bob and Sly are thinking; wonder who they

are? No, don't look at the screen, focus on the mirror, keep writing. Scared? Moi? Terrified. Something's going to happen, and I don't like mirrors. Never did. When I was young I looked stupid in them, couldn't get one to fit. Joke. Now I just look kind of weird, old.

And yet, here *I* am and here *it* is—propped up against the screen and a small pile of books. It's a bit of a family heirloom, handed down from goodness knows who, reasonably large, rectangular and nicely deep. It's a good mirror, polished for the occasion, and a face is staring back at me; yes, still me... for the moment, and it's looking kind of stupid, shamefaced. It thinks I'm a moron. It knows I'd rather be somewhere else. And it is wrong. Tonight I'll know everything—either that there *is* nothing or that the Devil exists. And I will ask. And he will give.

I want to be rich, to breath money, have it oozing from my pores. I want the world. I want everything. I want my little boy to live. Can I have both?

The room is warm and comfortably gloomy. Daniel's bedroom is behind me, a shadowy blur behind my face, my reflection.

Is there a time-lapse between image and reflection do you reckon? Well, I mean there must be, but not so you'd notice. An hour or two ago, I probably felt the same as the face staring back at me. Except reflections lack feelings.

Don't they?

It may be the other way round, either that or a subtle transaction occurs. My reflection doesn't look how I feel. It's now watching *me*. There's hunger in its eyes. But I have witnesses, Simon and Bob, the Captain and Sly. Sly and the Captain. The child keeping time to its skipping.

I stare at the face, no longer mine but *the face*. It blurs in abstraction. A face shared is a face halved, and I wonder if Sly and Bob are staring as hard at mine. They should be safe enough. The legend has nothing about the devil being able to get you from over a webcam.

And why would he bother, with me glaring into his looking glass? I can wait. All night if I have to—or as long as the whiskey lasts. If he comes... well, you'll see the results, and you can tell me all about it if things go wrong, and I'm left drooling on a commode.

Zak. Why are you doing this?

"Bob, right? You know the story of Rumplestiltskin?"

Yeah, the guy who...

"The woman, moron..."

Right, the woman who bargained her future child so as to marry the prince. My mother read it to me.

You think it's a children's story... I suppose it is. Except no one really grows up, not really. We make the very same mistakes the stories warn against.

A mistake—so why are you here?

Bob's voice echoes across the room. My eye seemed to be staring into those of a stranger.

She sold her child for position. I'm selling myself for a child.

That's so cool. And you want nothing more.

He wants nothing more.

The voices overlap, creating a gloating dissonance. "Fuck's sake, you know I want more."

We know you want more.

What? Bob's voice.

I gulp whisky. I'm baring my soul to strangers. The Devil knows the state of it. Why should two strangers in distant dark rooms? Change the subject. Keep staring.

Do you two know what an obsession is? I don't mean what it says in dictionaries. I'm talking about the real thing. Have you ever been obsessed? When I was younger I found myself spooked by Isaac Newton.

The dude who ate apples?

Dropped them, you sucker, Bob crows.

The crazy fuck also inserted needles behind his eyes to test the optic nerve. I mean he experimented on himself.

Now *that's* obsession. He could have gone blind. Just the tiniest slip...

My own eyes are staring back with me like they belong to somebody else.

So what's your point, Zak?

What's my bloody point? What do you think *I'm* doing? This is me, sticking that goddamned needle behind my soul... putting it on a hook for his infernal majesty. Maybe he'll appear to the sound of African drums. ... *Please allow me to introduce myself...* Yeah, OK, dumb, dumb, dumb. And this is serious business, right? There's two bottles of whisky here to prove it. Beer is cheaper but I'd be on the toilet all night, and the whole point of this is to stay here, in full view of you guys; me staring at a face I can no longer stand, these little fingers of mine tapping away, and you and anyone else watching.

Maybe nothing will happen, apart from a hangover and repetitive wrist injury. That would be something, right? Only you know what? I don't think it's going to turn out that way. Something is going to happen tonight. I know it. By the pricking of my thumbs... and all that crap.

You need to be honest with us, Zak. Captain Bob abhors evasions. The voice sounds sinister. I don't know Captain Bob. How did he find me? What's he doing here?

That's right, Zak. Tell us about Rumplestiltskin again.

They're frightening me, those voices.

Only because we don't buy that obsession crap. Me and Sly, we understand obsessions. You were changing the subject.

The face in the mirror shifts. Its mouth opens. It says one word. "Blood."

Blood for wealth and power.

Fame.

Now we're talking, Zak.

The Devil deals in blood... as down payment.

You make him sound a bit of a monster there, Zak.

Sly chuckles. *Not the master of urbanity we know and admire.*

Master of urbanity—a nice touch. You know ancient cities were built on blood.

Ah, the child in the stones.

Even London. It's wired in us. We know who rules this world... how you can get anything... if you're prepared to pay the one who rules it.

Souls.

Blood.

Fame swims in blood.

Stalin... Oh Captain Bob likes Stalin.

Genghis ...

Hell, even Lincoln. Politicians, maybe they do it for themselves, and maybe they pay the price for the rest of us. And then there's artists and rock stars, footballers. They paid the price—else someone close to them.

And what price will you pay, Zak?

They say mirrors open doors to Lucifer.

Changing the subject again. Bob sounds amused. I imagine him waving a finger.

They say? They say? Who says, Zak? Who the fuck says?

He's changing the subject, Sly.

The two speak as one. *What price will you pay, Zak?*

Does anyone worship the devil or are we all now part of him? I mean think about it for a moment; what chance do we have... did we ever have? These precious souls of ours, fluttering candles lost in a firestorm. I guess we're lost before we're born. We live in his world.

You're getting heavy again, Zak? But you still haven't told us why you're so desperate to see him.

He mentioned Daniel earlier on.

Oh, yes, he did. He did.

Daniel, Daniel, my beautiful son. Not so beautiful now. All these years, the years yet to come. You smile at me when you can. Do you forgive me?

Do you see anything yet, apart from yourself in that mirror?

Not yet, but the night's barely started. All I can see is what you're seeing, but from a different angle. A reflection.

And does it look like you?

I don't know anymore. Does it look like me? Receding hair, brown turning to grey. I touch my skin. In the mirror it looks dry. It feels damp. Sweat. Fear or an over-hot room. I stare more closely, real close, and see a thousand crossroads for the devil to choose from. They're thickest around the eyes and mouth. And there's one really deep wrinkle that plunges ink-like right down to my nostrils. It's a strong nose made bigger by the angle of the mirror.

And below—the mouth. The mouth? Shit, I'm writing like it doesn't belong to me. The mouth frowns back at me; and don't tell me mouths can't frown. Mine does. The lips pull down at the end, disapproval maybe, or disappointment, perhaps both.

I avoid the eyes. The mouth just frowns. But the eyes, I don't want to stare into them now. They hurt too much.

Look into them.

Fuck you. I stare at the face, blurring them out. Have you ever tried pouring whisky, and keeping eye contact with your reflection, afraid that it will spill it before you? All of us are shadows, reflections of others ceaselessly fading into alternatives, and only the face bears witness... see the whisky is taking effect. I'm speaking in tongues. I'm speaking double-Dutch. I'm fading... No, not yet. I must stay focused. What was I saying... only the face bears witness?

The face I wore as a child... is still there, somewhere, doing much the same thing I'm doing now... the earnest kid with large black glasses who went to confession on a Saturday and in the week gambled his soul.

Pardon me?

Don't laugh. I bet I wasn't the only one. I mean, has there ever been a survey done. Do you know?

You're losing me now, Zak

Celestial Blackjack. I used to promise my soul to the Devil if I stepped on a pavement crack. It would sometimes take me an hour to get to school, because you know what, as soon as I struck the deal the damned cracks thickened and spread.

And you never stepped on a crack?

I can still see them, those pavements, each with its patina of hairline fractures, waiting; just waiting.

And you never stepped on a crack?

No.

But you stepped on your son.

I dropped him. I was drunk. Daniel fell from a window.

I'm sorry.

It was a long time ago.

And children die, Zak.

He didn't die. He's in the bedroom behind me. He's in pain—always in pain.

And so you call Lucifer.

I've tried calling God. One gives me nothing. I'm going for bust.

Look into your eyes, Zak. Look into the eyes.

And see the devil staring back at me. That's what you're saying. I'm not ready. If I just lose focus for a moment my face kind of blurs into something more agreeable; abstract. The eyes disappear. Maybe the devil will emerge from the mottled smear of flesh and shadow... re-focus... focus... something was there. Oh God... Oh God... Something was there. Something was really there. Focus on the face. Sharp. Strong. My face. The eyes.

What's happening?

I don't know. The mind plays tricks.

But faces?

They stand guard over what we are—what we were. Still

staring at mine... It guards my past, my son. *His* face when it happened. The memory is strong, drawing me... daring me to...

What do you really want? The voice fills the room. It comes from the mirror.

There's the big question. Bob sounds amused.

What do I really I want. I want Daniel as he was, happy. I want to make up the lost years. I want wealth. I want everything.

Your soul for Daniel.
My soul for Daniel.
And whose blood?
Can't be Zak's.
He's going for bust
Fame and good fortune
Freedom from care.

The voices patter like a ball on a wall, a child keeping time to its skipping. "It doesn't make sense!" I shout the words out, no longer typing. "It doesn't make sense."

It does to us. Happens more than you know.

It does to you, too. Look at yourself. Sly seems terribly close.

The mirror wobbles. My face wobbles with it. The whisky is gone.

We are with you, Zak.
All the way.

Yeah, right. I'm at the door, the voices following me, seeping through shadow. The walls seem flimsy, the door insubstantial.

Are you regretting this, Zak?

Am I regretting this? I feel numb but that's all. The line is in front of me, simple to stand on or step over. Bob and Sly are gone, but hands push from behind, one step and then another ... so easy ... such an obvious, necessary thing.

There's a reflection in the mirror over his bed and I look away quickly. I step forward, and the line cuts through me like a wire slicing cheese and something dies.

    Daniel's eyes open. He's too tired to speak, but his eyes, they shine in forgiveness and pain. The pillow rolls over his face, and his struggle is short. A blood price. His happiness... and mine.

Senectus

Latin is not a dead language.

"You've known this from the start... I don't understand." Only Jack did understand. The problem was what to do about it. He stared at her, waiting for the words to come. "Shelagh..."

She eased herself to the side of the bed, shrugged on a blouse. "I know what you're thinking, and yes, you're right. My parents have been going on to me ever since they found out. I mean, Jack—you're going to be shot." Her eyes widened as though it had already happened.

"Lots of people get shot, no... I mean..." What did he mean? "It doesn't say when. Who's to say I don't get shot in a nursing home?"

She looked at him pityingly. "Exactly, Jack. Old people don't get shot. Young people do. I mean, I'm going to die in old age, and like, you'll have been dead for years."

"I told you on our first date." His voice sounded weak, almost petulant.

"Yes, but I didn't know you then."

"I'm sorry, Shelagh. Is there logic in there somewhere?"

She ignored him. "It's not just my parents. I don't want a child without a father. I don't want to be a bloody widow. I don't."

I don't want... I don't want. And I don't want a whiny tin-brained woman... only he did. He loved her. He loved her to death. He smiled at the thought. "So what was it your parents said? No, don't bother I can guess." He fingered the chip-scar behind his left ear.

It told anyone all that needed to be known about him, including the manner of his death. Everyone had one. It came with the first vaccinations: rubella, tetanus—and the 'but *you* don't need to bother with these because you're going to die in a plane crash / get shot / drown at sea / commit suicide chip'. Only he knew he wouldn't commit suicide. Not unless it involved shooting himself.

Shelagh had dressed now and was kneeling on the bed, her face inches from his. He loved her smell, her full, slightly sulky lips, and how they felt when they touched his. Like they were now. He pushed his tongue in between them and she drew back.

"I'm sorry, Jack." She held his shoulders. "I hope you find someone."

"Yeah, like maybe I'll put an ad in Psycho Weekly. Wanted: Dom. Femme. Must love guns."

She hadn't answered his question though. What had her parents said? He sighed and stooped to where his trousers lay on the floor. It didn't matter. He could guess. New hierarchies were forming. In a distant past it had been land, later money, then genetics. And now this: folk-myth and superstition that offered the illusion of control.

He pictured Shelagh's mother saying in that smooth, calm voice of hers that Jack had no future; that it wasn't fair on the children. It was middleclass garbage, based on the wisdom that those conceived in 'violent-death' families would inherit the same unfortunate traits. Marital alliances of the 'blessed' were things families strived for. It was snobbery pure and simple, and when you were dealing with that, all the statistics in the world were things to be argued over or ignored.

She saw him to the door, hand resting gently on his shoulder... even her touch made him burn. He didn't know whether to hit her or cry. Outside the street was black in rain.

He stepped quickly in to the shadows. Newport was dangerous in darkness. The road led down to marsh and Pill-shanty where small stilted buildings co-existed with even smaller houseboats further beyond. It was the same in most cities, even worse in the big ones. London, Manchester, Birmingham, all of them belonged to the gangs at night.

Simon pushed his glasses up closer to his eyes; looked at the figures once more, and sighed. He put them to one side and picked up the tumbler. It was two thirds full of whisky. As he'd said to his wife, his death wouldn't be drink related. Even so he cleaned glasses scrupulously and used only bottled water for ice. He closed his eyes the figures clear in his mind. It was a holocaust. No other word would suffice. The question was Jack. What part would his son play in the horrors to come?

He transferred the drink to his other hand and stretched out so his fingers touched the file he'd just discarded. He couldn't just put it to one side nor would governments, here or abroad. He compiled statistics; governments turned them into lies. He wondered what they'd do with these. What would he tell Jack? It was an empty question. He knew the answer to that one. Nothing.

How did you tell someone that death on an unimaginable scale was less than a decade away? Fire and murder—bombings—explosions—gunfire—a biblical winnowing. At least Jack wouldn't be alone when the bullets came. The figures for 'projected violent death' had been rising for some time not only here but across the world... but on this scale...?

He stared across the dimly lit room then closed his eyes again, seeing now not the figures but countless newly chipped babies sharing a common blood-filled destiny. The figures made him physically sick. A geometric increase had become a tsunami. They had to be wrong, but the figures had been checked and double-checked and the Crystal didn't make mistakes.

It must mean war. What else could it mean? The great continents skimmed through his mind: America, Europe, Asia, Africa, Australia... the figures had been universal: Bloodshed and violence. He wondered what the governments would say and, more importantly, what they would do. He raised the glass to his lips and finished it in a gulp.

Once, statistics had measured the past. Since the discovery of the alien artefact, they now mapped out futures. He glanced at the obsidian sphere on his desk, a facsimile provided by the insurance agency that had granted him cover at a cost he could barely afford. The Crystal Program was responsible for that, responsible for much he abhorred.

His gaze switched back to the discarded file. The figures were accurate. They might equally be self-fulfilling. Government would analyse and argue and eventually prepare for war. They had to. It was what governments did, and with less evidence than this. His wife, a philosopher of the cynical school had called it 'pursuing the inevitable'.

He smiled at the memory and recalled her laughter at the Korean experience. Was it the north, or the south? He couldn't remember, but he imagined the bureaucrat who'd first dreamt it up, someone with a precise and oriental mind. It was in the early days of Crystal, back when people were still trying to understand the implications, not realising then that they were of the kind you couldn't plan for.

The idea was simple and stupid—however you played it. Its first incarnation was to conscript all those predestined a violent death but with generous benefits for their dependents. It was neat. It saved on pensions along with hospital bills, but it had one fatal flaw. Morale hit rock bottom. Depression was rife, and the lesson was learnt, almost too late. No one likes death-heads, never mind buddying up to them in a trench.

The other way of playing it was to create 'non-fatality' regiments; those destined to die from liver disease or emphysema. Pursuing the inevitable Kathy had called it, and she'd laughed even louder. Caught in conflict these battalions had cooperated with what was predicted for them by surrendering or fleeing the field. Either way it did little good to anticipate outcomes. Things happened as they happened. Whatever the government did or didn't do, an unimaginable carnage was on the way.

"Dad?"

He hadn't heard the door open. "Jack, I'm in here."

"Where's the whisky?"

"That's in here, too."

"Bad day at the Stats Office?" It was usually said as a joke, as though nothing really bad could happen in a place so barren. This time the tone was different. Flat. Jack's face peered through the opening to the study. He looked miserable, angry.

"You OK?" Simon pointed to the half empty bottle. There was another behind it. "You can have your own if you want?"

Jack nodded and took the half empty bottle. "Shelagh's dumped me."

"Because...?" Simon cocked his head to one side waiting for what he expected to hear. It broke his heart. Kathy's death had been bad enough. Expecting it every time she left the house was even worse. Died in the line of duty the citation said. There was a letter, too, from the Chief Constable with words like '... extraordinary police officer... extraordinary courage'. It said nothing about a husband who'd had to anticipate it every day of his married life, of a son who had never been told until it was too late. And now this.

"Because... bloody because." Jack swilled whisky around his glass.

"She doesn't want what we've been through." Simon drew in breath and released it in a heavy sigh. It hurt him when his son was hurt. It hurt him knowing his wife's death was not the end of it. One day his son would also be shot. That was the worse of it—knowing.

Simon grimaced, sipping the whisky more slowly than usual. His own death was far more prosaic. Food poisoning. Prosaic but with consequences: travel insurance was barely affordable, and he never ate out. Consequences you could build a life around. He glanced at the file on the table beside him. A sin of omission ... another one. Let him find out in his own time, not now.

"Jack... you will find someone."

The lane was deserted. Jack walked cautiously, aware that even here someone might be waiting. To his left, cows grazed in deep green meadows, some ambling over to the hedge. He slowed and then stopped, allowing them to approach. They stared at him with that peculiar cow look: incurious but churlish, as though possessed of some collective intuition of how they were to die and who was responsible. Only sometimes they got their revenge. It was a cow that'd killed his father. BSE. Food poisoning of a kind though not what they'd expected.

He raised his hand to stroke the head of the nearest beast. It backed away, its eyes dull in resentment and hurt. It knew its fate... like all of them. People and cows... only people were less passive. They went berserk.

Jack smiled. His father had anticipated war, had tried to protect him from the inevitable. Only the inevitable had been misunderstood. Instead society had disintegrated. Humanity couldn't cope. A cocktail of despair, envy and sheer bloody-mindedness had spread virus-like, accelerating as governments responded in the way governments did. The worst was over, or so they said. He doubted it. Crystal had been stopped but there was still a generation out there waiting to die and raging against it.

He turned, looking down at the city he'd grown up in. Washed in a late afternoon sun, Newport glowed. It looked deceptively serene, a smaller version of the vast urban sprawls now straddling the planet. As he stood the boom of powerful guns broke the silence. Smoke hazed the sky over Ringland.

At night it was worse. Britain remained a patchwork of terror and fear, where big fish ate smaller fish, and safety lay in tribe and clan. The rich survived. They paid for security. They paid for Jack.

He checked his watch and continued walking up the lane. To his right lay woodland, broken by a narrow path. He turned into it, coming at last to a small clearing and a shed almost hidden in foliage and bramble. It was where he stored his bike, an armoured SUV and a variety of weapons, including an antiquated but effective AK 47. Monmouth was twenty-five minutes away. She wanted to be out of the country by this time tomorrow.

"You're still alive then?"

He couldn't believe it. "Shelagh."

She smiled and shrugged in the self-deprecating manner of the rich. "Didn't you know?"

"They said to look out for a Mrs Cunningham."

"I asked for you especially." She sounded pleased with herself.

He gazed about him. The manor was fortified and completely hidden from the road. "You've done yourself proud."

"No, I haven't," she said. "Not really." She flicked a wrist at the drive and the building behind her. "I've got this." Then she smiled. "Come in, you must be thirsty."

"Is there a Mr. Cunningham?"

"You mean—'am I in with a chance?' And the answer's yes, either way. Mr. Cunningham's not here." She touched his arm. "It'll be nice re-visiting old times."

He followed her into the house, watching the natural sway of her body, a red dress as tight as her skin. "You're going to have to do something."

She turned and smiled slowly. "What do you suggest?"

"I'm talking about tomorrow," he said. "Women aren't safe, even in daylight—especially where we're going."

"Oh." She grimaced and then shrugged. "I've got that in hand."

"You'll dress down?"

"Better than that."

He lay on the bed, her smell, the room dim in candlelight. He wondered where she was—what she was doing. The door opened slowly revealing a dark space where she should have been standing. "Shelagh?"

A boy walked into the room. He was dressed in denim, the jeans ill fitting, the shirt a size too big.

Jack rose from the bed and walked across the room. "Shelagh...? You look bloody awful."

She pouted. Moved closer. Without really thinking he stroked his finger down the side of her face, observed her head lean to one side as he reached her jaw and then neck. Her eyes closed. His hand returned to her shoulders. Too slender he thought, for a boy, the mouth too pretty. She'd done a good job with the hair though; it was short and choppy as if cut by a drunk and a very blunt knife.

"You didn't use to like boys."

"I don't."

"Good." She wriggled free from his grasp, and before he knew it her arms were about his neck. His slid down her back and waist, coming to rest on her bottom. He lifted her up, a hand on each buttock and swept her across the room to the bed. Her hands were hot, urgent, ripping through buttons, tearing at his shirt, working their way down to his waist and thighs. They lay on the bed half clothed, fighting for position, brazen and stupid, as though it was their first time and too drunk to care.

When they were done, it was Shelagh who pulled away. He stared at her body, yellow in candlelight, half-hidden in shadow. Her mouth was sullen, as though she hated who she was, what she was doing; her eyes were unreadable, a gleam in the dark.

"What's wrong?"

"You're still alive."

Jack winced. "That's the second time you said that. Should I feel guilty?"

"No."

Silence.

He saw her fists clench and when she spoke her voice was tight.

"I could scream for all those wasted years."

"Why don't you?"

She traced a finger down his chest and waist. "I mightn't be able to stop."

"That's a line."

"No," she said. "It isn't. I really do have everything—everything I thought I wanted except..."

Jack's gaze drifted across the darkened room. She wanted him.

"Peter—Cunningham—my husband... well, he isn't much of one."

"Children?"

"No—not yet."

"Maybe..." He stopped. After all this time, she wanted him back. Let her do the talking.

She shook her head; placed a finger on his lips and eased herself closer. He felt her hand on his chest, brushing softly down to his stomach, and then she straddled him, her knees hot, once more pressing into his thighs. He stared up at the small breasts hanging just over his mouth. She smiled sardonically, but her eyes shone. She looked drunk and happy, triumphant.

"Maybe, yes maybe."

The drive had been uneventful. She'd examined the vehicle carefully, stroking finger patterns in its camouflage of grime. "It's a beautiful vehicle," she said, "underneath the filth."

"The filth's its first line of defence," he said. "Beneath that it's plate steel and high-armoured glass. It'll take a grenade."

"To think Crystal did this."

You seemed to have escaped, he thought. "It killed my dad, watching my mum leaving for work... and then me. Everyday was a small death for him. The real one came as some relief."

"He was glad he died before you."

"Yes."

She shuddered. "My father used to tell me stories about Syria—long before this. I didn't believe him."

"And now they've come true ... and you're leaving." His voice was neutral, hiding the bitterness.

"Jack, you could come with us?"

She'd told him about St. Lucia in the early hours of the morning. It was part of the Barbadian federation they'd bought into. "And the best part of it, Jack, they're clean of people. It's the nearest thing to paradise on Earth, and you could be part of it, Jack. Peter wouldn't mind, and we..." She giggled. "We could do what we do best."

God, she doesn't think she's 'people' now. "Only I'm still going to get shot."

"When I think of all those wasted years..."

"And," said Jack, ignoring her, "on balance, I think I'd rather be shot by a stranger than by an angry husband... It wouldn't do much for *your* reputation."

After that she said nothing.

The yacht, *Senectus,* was waiting at Malpas Quay, where

she'd promised it would be. He was grateful for that. He didn't want to hang around.

"Strange name."

"What? Oh, the yacht. It's Peter's—sixty last year. He bought it for himself."

He helped her with her various bags, most of them antique Vuitton, and more expensive than anything she had in them. Someone in a striped vest took them away and for a moment they stood there, searching for whatever it was they wanted to say.

"A Casablanca moment," said Jack.

"What?"

"Nothing."

"What will happen to you?"

He looked back. "A sniper's bullet probably. And you?" He remembered—one of the lucky ones—Shelagh would die in old age.

"A husband. She patted her stomach. "Perhaps something more."

He looked at the yacht. *Senectus*. He wondered what it meant. "Who knows? You always were the lucky one."

Ailsa

How long does a Were-beast live?

"He's late," Monty said. "Should have been here by now."

Will understood her worry. The crowd was quite good—especially considering the author was a relative unknown and came from Canada. 'Bit of a cult figure,' Will had assured her. 'Word will get round.' And it had. That was the problem. The people were here. The author was missing.

A blast of cold air and a splatter of rain caused several to turn. Monty rose, relief evident in her manner and face. "He's here."

"And about bloody time." Will shifted in his seat and glimpsed a shaggy, bearded man muscling his way through the bar. He looked much like his photographs but more bad tempered.

Monty's head barely reached his chest but she guided him like an imperious terrier to the lectern and the thick crescent of chairs almost surrounding it. As he passed, Will caught a distinct whiff of wet dog and a deeper, more unpleasant smell. He remarked on it after Monty, introductions made, returned to her seat.

"He's a bit whiffy, don't you think?"

"Maybe his smell has a cult following too. Though actually, I found it quite nice—musky... very masculine."

Will settled back, aware that the speaker was staring at them, as though he heard every word and was considering a response. He cleared his throat: "My name is Neill Edward, but then you know that. I've just been introduced." A flicker of polite laughter and then silence.

Will sensed curiosity, a willingness to be entertained and uncertainty, too. Probably the accent, the sheer size of the man, his red lumberjack shirt with cut-off sleeves, the tattoos crawling up his arms and neck. Teeth were a bit of a state too. Heroin, he guessed.

"This is a story I wrote some time ago. Set in the Dark Ages. Love gone wrong. You might call it autobiographical." He grinned as though he'd just made a joke and then coughed:

Rhiona stood on the beach, a small, thin figure. She didn't wave or move but Ailsa felt her resentment. Rhiona wanted them, Niall most of all. Niall she had loved. Ailsa grimaced. Her mother loved him more than her. She had no doubt about that. Ailsa watched her, a diminishing speck upon a thin line of sand.

The curragh glided over the gentle swell of the bay. A scream of gulls rose about them, wheeling and weaving in the raw wind. Ailsa stared over the bows, seeing very little. They were sailing into a thickening mist, as if someone or something was intent on hindering them. Within moments, Riona's village faded into a murky half-light: sea, land and sky, seeping in to a dull, grey equivalence.

She gazed down at Niall, still peacefully asleep beneath the foul smelling wolf-skin. She replaced it with a rug, stowed the skin in her bag. They were sailing west to the home of the sun, the Isles of the Blessed. Escape.

Her gaze switched to the rest of the crew coming to terms with an unfamiliar craft. Cadmun had accepted at once, patting his harp enclosed in oiled leather Rorin and Brin had spent a night talking about it. None of them remembered everything, but enough to make them glad to be sailing west.

The ship twisted, forcing Ailsa to tighten her grip on the steering paddle. Balance was everything. Kept level, the curragh would skim the surface like a feeding tern.

Above her the great hide sail sucked and slapped, trapping the wind and throwing it back. Its shadow loomed over all of them, their immediate fate resting in its capacity to mould gale and storm.

Gradually the mist thinned into an empty sea, a white featureless sky, and a swell that was taking them nowhere, slowly. Ailsa sighed. She wondered when the change would take place, whether Niall would still love her, love her enough. She wondered when, if ever, he'd eventually awake.

Ailsa extended a foot. She gave Niall a hopeful kick. No response. Gloomily she returned to a rudder that seemed able to sense any sign of distraction.

Niall had once warned them, the boat was alive, an animal as wild as the sea, a living, breathing sentient being. Ailsa agreed. They were immersed in a world of emptiness and sound: the slap of breaking waves, the creaks and groans of leather and wood. She glanced across the heavily greased ship, aware of its sides breathing gently, at one with the sea.

A fierce punch almost knocked her over the side of the curragh. Instinctively her hand reached out to grasp one of the sail ropes and she turned to see Niall's maniacal face grinning down at her.

A roaring cackle filled the night air.

Ailsa stepped back, for a moment unsure, then Niall thumped her again, this time on the arm.

"It's good to be back." He looked across the sleeping boat. "And at sea, too."

"How are you feeling?"

"Like I've been to Hell and back. I feel... I feel..." Niall paused to examine himself. "I don't know how I feel." Then he stopped, his heavily tattooed face assuming a more sombre cast. "Ailsa, I remember nothing."

Ailsa stared silently at the Attacotti scout. "You remember me."

"Yes... I love you..." He turned, gazing back at the ship's wake. "It's there I cannot remember. And why we are here."

How much to tell him? "We where held by a witch, Niall. She held you in thrall—wanted to kill me... to kill us all in time." *No need to tell him the witch was her mother or that...* She shook her head. No, he'd find out eventually.

"So how did we escape?" He looked over the ship's bow and then at the sky.

"I sold a part of me in order to free you ... to free us all."

He looked at her sharply. "Words, Ailsa. What did you do?"

I drugged you and your crew, killed men as they slumbered, stole something my mother valued even more than you. "Deceit," she said, "and a drink that brings sleep."

Niall nodded as though he understood. "And you stole us a boat."

"We sail where you intended ... before you found our village."

"Tir n'an Og, I remember ... I take it you drugged our wine."

Ailsa smiled. "And you drank more than your fill."

Niall growled and shook his head.

"So, the hero awakes?" A face emerged from a bundle of fur.

Niall stared at him, his face impassive. "And who the shit are you?"

Cadmun grinned. "He's sounding better, too—last time he was awake, he was screwing a witch and eating *her* shit."

Niall narrowed his eyes, inclining his head to one side as if sizing up a horse, or an enemy, then, unexpectedly, he laughed. "Shit is shit. I remember now." He stared along the curved ship to where Rorin and Brin lay sleeping, gazed for a moment at Ailsa, then turned to where Cadmun was slowly stretching, breathing in the early morning light. "At least I think I remember. You are Cadmun, a bard. You owe me a song."

The bard laughed, without humour. "And people might sing it one day."

"Probably not," said Ailsa. She glanced at Niall. The Attacotti was shaking his head slowly from side to side then faster and faster, teeth bared, his hair-tail swinging. He stopped abruptly and winced. "There is too much in my head to clear. "Tir n'an Og—we're all agreed?"

"Tir n'an Og welcomes heroes," said Cadmun.

"Not those that are ravenous," Niall said, looking at each in turn. His smile revealed blackened teeth, eyes that sparkled like blue stars. "Morrigan's teeth, but I'm hungry!"

Days followed days. The nights brought no respite; a succession of foul, black squalls and driving rain reduced the visible world to the low heaving sway of a wood and leather shell. Regardless of their efforts, the curragh was sinking lower into the swell. Water swirled ominously in the well of the craft. The smallest wave slopped over the prow. And yet, despite a surface gloom, Niall continued to exude an underlying stubborn cheerfulness. "It will be better tomorrow," was a constant refrain and on the fourth day, he was proved right.

They worked that day, baling the ship dry, knotting down everything moveable, and caulking, greasing, replacing frayed ropes. That night they slept, the steer-paddle tied, unmanned. They slept like dead men. The following day the weather changed again.

Niall pointed to a horizon deep in cloud, bearing down upon them. The curragh rolled heavily under and over an ominous swell. His response was laconic. "Now we're in trouble."

Rorin squinted at the approaching storm. Huge waves were advancing upon them, a mountain range of water enraged by wind and current. He squeezed Brin's shoulder, as if in encouragement. The older man grimaced, his jaw taut. "Well tell us what to do then," he shouted. His hair whirled and fluttered, streaming behind him like an icy tail; his voice was faint, consumed in the wind.

"Take down the sail! Rorin!" Niall pointed. "You and Cadmun tie down the tents—tie down everything that moves. Brin, you help too. Ailsa..."

"I know. Stick firm to the rudder."

Niall gave a maniac's grin. "I was going to say hold tight."

The storm advanced relentlessly, the sea now a looming avalanche, each wave swelling, heaving into fast moving mountains rearing high into the sky. And every time the fractional pause before a roar of dark glassy green slammed into the boat.

Ailsa hung grimly onto the steering paddle, for support rather than in any hope of control. It was like being pounded by hammers, each stroke exploding into a chaos of foam and spray.

"Ailsa!"

Ailsa caught a flicker of movement. A rogue wave had erupted from nowhere and was advancing at right angles upon the curragh, its crest towering over the mainmast—toppling—engulfing. Ailsa jerked at the steering paddle, swinging the boat round. She felt the prow rearing up behind her, struggled against the wrenching force that threatened to topple them into the sea.

No sooner had she caught her balance than another vast wave swelled, taunting the fragile beetle of a curragh to climb yet another green relentless face. A sickening pause - teetering on its brink - then the slow yawn forward, sliding down into the trough, another wave breaking over them as they descended. A great wall of water submerged the sky, and they found themselves immersed in ocean.

The curragh wheeled crazily, pressing deep into troughs the size of canyons, crashing through ravenous slabs of wet solidity, then riding buoyant on brief impossible peaks before another stomach-churning drop into the maelstrom.

Ailsa felt her face melting under the unrelenting spray, her friends barely a blur in the sting of brine. Somewhere in the storm she heard a series of wild, piercing shrieks and knew it was Niall, laughing. She glimpsed him, capering between mast and ropes like some aquatic goat, exulting, knowing they could do little, content to be as one with the storm. Guiding and controlling its outcome or accepting destruction was equally agreeable to him. It was why she loved him.

"Ailsa!"

Again the warning cry, and again desperate, instinctive evasion. A great slope of water yawned to envelop them and in the dark swirl they heard mountains roar and crash, then disintegrate into spray and air. And again the curragh prevailed, lurching and plunging through a storm that wouldn't end. Now Niall's laughter was no longer heard, and Ailsa wondered how many of them would survive the gale.

Ailsa awoke before dawn to the sound of rolling thunder, the hiss of rain on hide. She picked her way through the sleeping bodies and peered into an iron-grey dimness. For a time she could see little and so listened, remembering the force and fury that had come and gone. She stared into the darkness, remembering. Pictures formed in her mind, trees emerging slowly around her ...

There is a path of sorts of branches and bracken. Ailsa hesitates then walks into the forest. She slithers on thick smears of mud and snow, scrabbles for balance... a clearing ... In its centre is a small lean-to of branches and tanned leather. Surrounding it are four poles upon which hang a collection of skulls. She raises the flap and enters.

The floor slopes sharply into a large underground chamber covered in skins. At its centre is a small fire that burns brightly and without smoke. A man sits there, still like stone. He wears a mask of leather and wood; it is fringed with stems and fresh green leaves. Two black oval shapes indicate where eyes should be, but none are visible in the shadow behind the mask.

Ailsa knows what he is: a witch like her mother, only stronger. She waits patiently and then the shaman raises his head, quietly directing her to the hearth. Still nothing is said. Ailsa sits, feeling numbed by fire and snow. There is no going back.

The shaman speaks. "You know the price?"

"I do."

"A price you are willing to pay?"

"Yes."

"And you have brought the skin." It wasn't a question.

Ailsa nodded. "I took it from my mother."

"As she took it from hers. Put it around you."

The great bear had come from the sea, its pelt as white as ice and snow. Now there was only fur, faded yellow from tallow and smoke.

The shaman offers her a goblet, brimming with something dark and red.

Ailsa inclines her head. She stretches over fire, grasps the offered cup, and drinks it quickly. It tastes warm and sticky, a dark unwholesome wine.

"The bear will come to you. He will grant what you most desire and take something in return."

Ailsa collapses. She is in her father's stables surrounded by childhood sounds, the snuffle of dogs hunting rats in straw, a slow breathing, the stolid chomp of horses. She hears her father's voice, the sound of someone laughing, her mother—before she changed. There is wetness on her face... salt on her tongue, and a voice telling her to let go... let go...

Her mind is free, a leaf on a river dissolving in vastness. She is a spark... a seed, vulnerable to the predatory beaks surrounding her. There is a ripple in the darkness, a supple flash, a lithesome red, and the figure of a man stares down at her. Broad lips curl, and a hand reaches out. Crimson fingers cup her in a palm as smooth as marble, and the demon yawns like a virulent sky, bringing with it the smell of honey and iron. His voice is an avalanche.

"Your friends will be saved Ailsa, and in exchange you will be my creature and I your master, and I will ride you through land and sea."

She shivers, knows there is more. She waits.

"You will bring me Niall. He, too, will wear the skin. You agree."

It isn't a question. She nods.

"You will try to evade me but I will be with you, until it is done."

The vision fades; the demon's eyes, dim suns in a vanishing night. She wriggles, impotent, a worm on a hook;

sees herself reflected, twice trapped in that ancient stare. Words echo in her head. 'You... will bring... me Niall. He... will wear... the skin.' They yelp and bay, chasing each other, like hounds at play.

"Ailsa..."

Over the fire the shaman's eyes burn through the mask like torches to another world, a gateway world, bounded by voids and demons and gods.

"...You have had your answer."

The room is cold, the shaman's breath pale wisps, seeping out from a green and leathery mask, vanishing in the now freezing air. Ailsa struggles to open her eyes. Her bones ache from damp...

"So we're still here then?" Niall brushed back his hair and soothed his beard as if it were a cat or something more wild. When no answer came, he jerked himself up with a groan and joined Ailsa at the ship's prow.

"You're thinking about the storm?"

Ailsa shook her head.

Niall looked at her. "What then?"

And Ailsa told him, omitting only her final promise.

"Do you still have the skin?"

Ailsa managed a pale smile. "I left it behind... with the men I killed."

"Then he is no longer in you."

"I don't know. Sometimes I awake, sensing his fury. But when I listen there is only the sound of the sea."

"You don't sound convinced."

"His memory is in me. Is that the same?"

Niall shrugged, fingered his sword. "He made you his creature."

Niall, he thinks of killing me.

"What will be, will be, Ailsa." He shuddered. "What is it like...?"

"When the bear takes me?" Ailsa paused, collecting her thoughts. "He fills me with appetite. I see through his eyes. Dream his dreams. He would remake me, Niall... I fear what I might become."

Niall spoke, his voice low. "And you did this for me."

Ailsa stared at him briefly. "I remember waking afterwards. The Shaman was gone but demon was in me. Even then, I felt myself changing. I woke up in the forest, boiling with hatred and rage. But now it's not there ... all that rage. It's something I remember, but no longer feel."

"You think to escape?"

"If we sail far enough—find Tir n'an Og." Her shoulders slumped. "I don't know."

Niall shook his head, the loosely plaited hair swinging from side to side. "It's a dangerous business cheating a god, Ailsa. Sometimes they'll play a man like a fish."

He is still fishing. She grimaced. *With me as the hook.* "I know. Sometimes it's almost as if he were on board with us. He has a smell, Niall, and I look round expecting to see him, but then the smell vanishes, lost in salt, the reek of wool and sweat, and one of you is staring at me as though I have become suddenly witless."

Niall regarded her sombrely. "What's this smell like?"

Ailsa closed her eyes. "The stink of hot iron... sulphur perhaps, and something else, something terribly sweet." She opened them to find Niall had edged closer. "And it was here with us last night. It almost made me choke."

"Is that what woke you?"

Ailsa nodded. She felt shame. "I hoped for a moment it was one of you."

"You thought one of us might be harbouring this demon?"

Again, Ailsa nodded. "I crawled over each of you in turn, smelling -"

"Smelling our fragrance." Niall grinned. "It's a wonder you're still alive." His mood darkened. "Then we haven't escaped."

Night swept over them, tenting the curragh in darkness. Moonlight glittered on black water, the boat rocking gently to the cuff of an occasional wave.

"I see you can't sleep." It was Niall.

Ailsa nodded and yawned, then peered into the sky, seeking the star that guided them. The wind was warm, wet; a southerly, she thought. The curragh bobbed gently, lurching to the side on the occasional wave, its taut, greased skin, dampening the ripple and slap of an invisible sea. If she shut her eyes... the sensation was akin to being drunk, the body dissolving into a dark oceanic sway.

"Are you comfortable?" Niall asked dryly.

Ailsa hauled herself up. "I don't think we'll reach Tir n'an Og."

Niall paused before answering. "I know…"

Ailsa stared at him, stony-faced. "No you don't."

Niall grinned. "If you say so."

"Niall, I'm going to leave you … but first you must listen." That night she told him everything, what the Bear-demon wanted, showed him the skin.

"You think Rhiona killed your father."

"Like I might kill you."

"Unless I choose…" Niall glanced sideways at a cluster of stars that seemed to shine with a peculiar intensity. He pointed upwards; then, as Ailsa followed his gaze, pointed down to where they could be seen reflected, almost as brightly in the shifting sea. "There are many lands in Tir n'an Og, some only entered through death." He turned again towards Ailsa. His voice held mischief and sadness. "If we should meet there I will take you to an island most highly recommended." He paused, smiling wickedly. "It is inhabited by seventeen lubricious nymphs who'll satisfy your every need... And after they have done that they will discover in you needs no woman has ever before imagined."

Ailsa lay back, her eyes scanning the stars. "Your world is full of such stories, Niall."

"And yours." He thrust his hand over the rim of the curragh, watching the spray turn silver as the moon caught it in its light. He cupped his hand and tossed a handful of water into the blackness. "But I will not leave you."

Ailsa didn't reply. Where land met sea strange forces shaped how men thought, how Niall thought in his private world of magic and flux. Now they were lost in the source of that magic, the western ocean, in search of death or a life alone. Together they sat, all talking done, content to watch the approaching dawn.

A thickened sea rolled sluggishly about them, black and purple against the early morning light. An already fierce sun hit the water, bestowing upon each ripple and crest a rich, golden glow. Niall and Ailsa stared at the blazing water that held them tight.

"I'll keep you company." Ailsa squatted besides him, arranged the yellowing fur around his shoulders. An empty cup rolled between his feet.

"When will it happen?"

Ailsa shrugged.

"And how will I know?"

"You will smell only blood. It's then we must leave."

Niall nodded. If the timing was wrong they would die but their companions would live.

They sat for a while in silence. Every so often Niall glanced across at the hide sail, taut in a light wind and blocking out half the sky. His fingers drummed restlessly against the leather. Unable to sleep, he made his way to the prow, feeling the spray on his face. He peered through the mist, which shone white in the night. They were heading towards ice.

The boat shifted violently. Niall whirled round, his eyes focussing on the two irregularly shaped tents behind the mast. At first he saw nothing and then... The thing was crouched in a pool of shadow. A cloud shifted and in the bright moonlight, Niall saw more than his mind could hold. He closed his eyes quickly, and pressed himself against the prow. The icy slap of sea on leather called out to him. He felt its call, resisted it.

The creature grunted, as though trying to speak. Niall trembled. They had discussed every option, and he had chosen...

Only now...?

He breathed slowly, trying to regain control, felt his heart pounding. When next he looked, the creature had shifted its position and was staring at him. Niall stopped breathing. His eyes remained open. Like a rabbit caught in the flare of a torch.

The thing would have him in three or four bounds, and yet it remained still. Niall dared to breathe, keeping his eyes fixed on the beast that now emerged from the shadows. It was larger than any man, unnaturally large, as though its bones were fast outgrowing the flesh that encased them. Joints and muscles bulged like knotted ropes, and fur glistened white in grease: Ailsa, her face bestial and gaunt.

A flap of leather broke the stillness, and two figures

emerged from the tent. Rorin and Brin, Cadmun close behind. The creature, almost without appearing to move, slipped deep into shadow. Niall drew his sword and sucked in air, prepared to shout warning. At the same time the wolf launched itself at the two men.

He saw in fragments: a flash of white, a large jaw opened wide, abnormally so, and teeth that belonged to no human face. Rorin had his sword half drawn. Brin's mouth open in a long, silent scream. Then the two of them vanished beneath the weight of the beast. He was aware of a splash. Cadmun had chosen to drown.

Niall rose to his feet, sword in hand. He felt as though he were in a dream, one that he might wake up from but until then bound by what he had to do. Almost before he knew it, he was halfway down the ship. Before the masthead he froze, lost in the horror of what was before him.

They were already dead, their limbs flapping lifelessly as the thing worked in a frenzy on open flesh. Blood splattered, a fine dark mist flecking the creature's hair, soaking into immense white shoulders. Niall struggled to grip his sword, and watched as the creature pressed further into first one body and then the other, its jaws tearing into sinew and flesh. The night was silent but for a hoarse and steady panting, the snap and scrunch of jaw on bone.

It was now or never, while the creature was lost in gluttonous frenzy. Niall edged slowly forward, all the time balancing the two opposing thoughts in his mind: to die like them or to accept Ailsa's demon. He screamed, despair and Ailsa's name equally mixed. No one would write their song, but the ocean was clean. Death would be quick. The creature was looking at him. Niall paused, breathing in the cold night air.

"Ailsa... ! Do you know who I am?" He raised his sword, its hilt slick with sweat. Then he threw it, watching it spin and vanish in the sea. It was, he knew, the only option. She would kill him... or he would change. He couldn't kill her.

Niall grinned, inching forward; first one step, then another. Ailsa stared at him, gaze fixed upon her final meal. She rose snarling, lips curled, moist and black like those of a dog. She moved now with an easy grace, the remains of her former friends flecked her neck and chest.

"Ailsa, do you know me?"

She stood, looking at Niall through eyes that held no light. Niall bowed his head, no longer able to accept what he saw: a thing less than human, muscular, deformed; its white fur streaked dark red. Through eyelids—fluttering—unable to open, he sensed it looming closer, its smell sour and reeking of blood. He imagined it, black against the moon, its elongated jaw, dropping, teeth gleaming, poised.

Something touched his shoulder. Niall tensed. In a moment the shadow was gone. A splash rocked the boat, a low guttural wail, and then silence. He glimpsed something white, coursing through the water with serpentine grace. Niall hesitated then dived in behind her. Man or beast he needed Ailsa, the blood he smelled in the ocean and lands beyond that.

He put the book to one side and lowered his head. A tear, sharp as a pearl and then gone. Will shook his head; a trick of the half-light, one obscured by eyebrows and beard, the heads of those who stood to applaud..

About The Author

Michael Keyton has cooked in hospital kitchens, worked in some of the dirtiest hotels in Wales, and played for a time in a semi-professional ceilidh band.

He taught history in a warm and challenging school, where he learnt the importance of 'story' and developed an abiding love of Newport.

You can find him on his blog, **Record of a Baffled Spirit** (baffledspirit.blogspot.co.uk).

Other Titles

Dark Fire

Raoul, a C12th adventurer rescues Simone, the daughter of the legendary witch Melusine. Raoul, realises his danger too late. He has rescued her but also fallen captive to a love he will never escape. Both are now hunted, but as their pursuers close in, Simone has one last trick up her sleeve: Dark Fire, a satanic paste activated by sexual magic that will transport them through time and space. The only proviso is that they must find each other again. The penalty for failure is eternal damnation.

In the C21st their future hangs in the balance for Raoul is now Ralph and married to Laura. Simone is trapped in the C17th as Verity Strong. Time is against them…

Reader Alert! When Verity swaps bodies with Ralph she understands what it is to be a man. Ralph, trapped in her body sees things differently. Worse he is trapped in the C17th… but Verity has a plan.

CLAY CROSS

When James Finn ran down the priestess daughter of a houngan in a Louisiana bayou, he never imagined the consequences. When Laura Finn begins a search for her husband, the nightmare begins. James Finn finds himself trapped in the persona of Clay Cross, a 1950's cold war warrior and misogynist private eye, a composite of every pulp novel he's ever read.

Clay Cross is a swirl of Voodoo, Noir, and mangled metaphors, its comic aspects coming from a 1950's private eye out of his time.

Cheyney, Behave!

Peter Cheyney: A Darker World

Between 1936 and 1951 Peter Cheyney wrote over forty books and was the highest paid novelist in Britain. In many respects he blazed a path for Ian Fleming and the brutal glamour of Bond. Today, Peter Cheyney is almost unknown, his books out of print.

'Cheyney Behave,' recaptures a lost world and provides an eye-opening analysis of a popular culture we might prefer to forget. The book examines the importance of cigarettes and alcohol in Cheyney's world, his attitude to 'pansies', racism, women, and the jaw-dropping sexism of his age. It analyses the significance of Cheyney's 'Dark' series in terms of war propaganda and how Cheyney accurately captured the effects of war on prevailing morality.

For those jaded by pilgrimages to Baker Street, Cheyney provides a welcome alternative. Most of his many heroes, villains and victims live in a very small area of London. Some are unwitting neighbours, and all jostle each other on the same roads and streets, ghosts in parallel worlds. These are mapped, allowing the reader to go on his or her own 'Cheyney walk.'

Printed in Great Britain
by Amazon